Not for Human Consumption

Craig Watson

Not for Human Consumption

Published by The Conrad Press in the United Kingdom 2021

Tel: +44(0)1227 472 874
www.theconradpress.com
info@theconradpress.com

ISBN 978-1-913567-68-2

Typesetting and Cover Design by: Charlotte Mouncey, www.bookstyle.co.uk
The Conrad Press logo was designed by Maria Priestley.

Printed and bound in Great Britain by Clays Ltd, Elcograf S.p.A.

I would like to thank my editor Jemma Gurr for her superb assistance with the creation of this book and for her editorial contributions.

1

It was a bitter dawn. Bereft of laughter. Bereft of joy. Bereft of spirit.

The freezing mist was rolling in again, drifting through the shadows and curling through the air over parked cars, street signs, and benches, creating strange ghost-like apparitions.

A beautiful russet fox in its thick winter coat caught in the glow of a streetlamp crouched low, shrouded in mist unperturbed. Transfixed, it seemed to yawn exposing its sharp fanged teeth as a gust of wind ruffled the hair on its back before disappearing down the subway.

Padding through the underpass it had to run the gauntlet past junkies and drunks on both sides of the tunnel. Men and women with addled brains. Collapsed veins. Abscesses about to burst. Mentally and physically damaged and deranged. Schizoids. Minds warped by psychosis, trapped in an insane Punch and Judy sideshow whose cries and moans echoed down the gloomy tunnel like a tormented spirit.

A man sitting on a blanket drank from a can as he looked at the fox hands shaking. You could only wonder how much he was aware of anything, as he rolled his bloodshot eyes that had witnessed so much pain, loss, and affliction.

There was a new arrival sitting on an upturned crate outside a white battered tent. He had a towel over his head and was sniffing from an aerosol can. He inhaled the spray and it took its numbing effect.

They were all on a long dark road, nameless and without end, and saw many a day through a thick mist of chaos marooned down here on the fringes of society.

Things never looked bleaker for Magda. Pregnant and addicted to drugs and alcohol, it seemed the world had forgotten about her and left her to rot like the rubbish at her feet.

Cheeks ruddy and eyes dilating, they shouted across the subway and glared at each other psychotically. Dirt and cuts itched against their emaciated limbs as they curled up into tight balls, shivering and slowly self-destructing in the cold morning air. Drenched in the slag of weather forecasts, trapped in a world of continuous insomnia as others slept, and sheltered inside their tents, unaware of the destruction of their bodies slowly prising apart in their sleep. Not really sleeping, but lazy and crippled from their anaesthetic, curled into their tight balls coiling the ugliness of their wounds.

Every fibre of Harry's being was screaming for mercy and begging for forgiveness. He sobbed, barely able to speak, gasping for breath and shaking apart. Perspiration was seeping from every pore, only he was frozen. Jolts charged through his poisoned body as he lay cowering. Fear gripped him as the voices inside his head grew louder.

Billy sat dribbling from his mouth, his eyeballs sucked up to the top of his head. Two women in business suits stood to the side some distance away from him, chatting and rubbishing him over their plastic cups of hot coffee, unblemished and well-nourished.

The industrial-strength detergents could do nothing to mask the stench down here as people slopped along the urine and rain-soaked floor, staring down to the end of the dark passage which followed that fox to where the cold light of dawn shone through the other side. The walls were daubed with the obscene etchings of sick, the roof was leaking, and shouts echoed between the constant drip dripping of the water and feet splashing to the puddles on the floor. The stripped lighting along the defaced cream tiled walls kept flickering on and off were a moth fluttered. A creature of beauty with soft delicate wings of green and purple in a dark world surrounded by dirt and filth.

Men and women lay curled up in blankets amongst the squalor. Men with dead eyes burning into your conscience and sad desperate eyes staring into your soul. The old Latvian was curled up like a mongrel on the concrete floor with matted hair and ripped clothes riddled with fleas. Blood was splattered over his face, with most of his teeth kicked out from his past adventures. He was slowly dying an ugly death.

Hideous-looking creatures with mangled features and mangled limbs. Grubby and twisted with a curvature of the spine and bent out of shape by life's pliers. Suffering from a hopeless condition of mind body and spirit, which so many pursued to the gates of insanity or death. Few here managed to escape from the twilight zone of madmen and even madder women.

Joyce slumped against the wall, invisible to the constant flow of human traffic pushing and shoving and running as fast as they could to get out of the place. She was slurring and her words rambled along, incoherent and nonsensical. As she sat on a pile of cardboard with a screaming baby in her arms, millions of shopping bags, fast food wrappers, and cartons, washed over the concrete floor towards her like a great plastic tidal surge.

The baby was shared and passed around like a parcel by others in a grotesque game of cat and mouse to pull on the heartstrings of caring but gullible passers-by. She made a fortune.

The day was breaking as the fox ran through the deluge of flying debris to reach the light at the end of the tunnel. Passing the once beautiful ginger-haired girl with the lesions on her face and away from the flow of people and away from the lost souls sitting on their blankets and away from the hundred yards of sleep like a small community and emerged from the darkness and into the light.

2

Danny saw the blood dripping to the floor from his cut temple. He felt the squirming inside his stomach expand as they went inside him, and his insides ached and rocked. He felt it stab. He felt it shoot out stinging like acid. It became hard, there ceased to be flesh. That thing inside his body, an instrument of torture. Like the stale heart inside his mouth, he tried to dislodge it with his mind, but he couldn't.

They carried on and his heart burst. One kept looking at him, eyes wide as saucers, mouth open, and hair flapping across his face as the other moved inside again. Nausea crept against Danny's lungs, adrenalin drooling into his brain he struggled to break free from their hold as they sunk themselves deeper inside him.

They left him. The door slammed and Danny watched a twenty-pound note gently float to the floor.

Danny's life had become a war zone. He had become damaged by the violence inflicted upon him. All feeling flooded from within him. Panic filled his heart and the punchbag that he had become groaned.

The day always began with the shakes. Sickness and fear. Paranoia, dry retches, dizziness, difficulty breathing, Sore eyes, dry mouth, banging head, aching limbs, raging hunger, anxiety, suicidal thoughts, the shits, chills, projectile vomiting, chronic diarrhoea, and stomach cramps, all of which only a *fix* would fix.

Danny could feel the bile rising from the pit of his stomach. He dragged himself up off the floor crawled into a cubicle bent over the edge of a cracked and blocked toilet bowl full to the rim with diarrhoea gagged and shook before letting go at both ends.

Blackout.

Sometime later, he regained consciousness.

Danny managed to stagger outside and onto the street. It was another soulless day, cast underneath a leaden sky.

Danny felt ashamed. His clothes were rags full of excrement urine and vomit, his body was bloodied and bruised, his face full of bruises and bumps, cuts, and scratches. Emerging from the old toilet block, the daylight stung his eyes. His head was fizzing, and everything was blurred and distorted like looking through a fairground mirror.

Yesterday's snow now formed streams of dirty brown slush on the pavement, which seeped through his split soled boots, held together with gorilla tape and dampening his socks.

Coming out of the toilet was a trial once more. You had to run the gauntlet of drunks and smackheads gathered outside their tents, viciously demanding money and cigarettes.

The bitter north wind whipped around their canvas tents, crying and moaning like a tormented spirit as it howled through their ramshackle encampment outside the old toilet block. Danny saw some people sitting on abandoned broken furniture, some on the ground, and some standing around a makeshift oil drum fire, like a small post-apocalyptic community.

Danny sat on the damp grass broke, broken, cold, and dying. Dying for a fix. His legs had gone stiff and the alcohol poisoning cramps had set in. The muscles in his legs spasming, sending shock waves of pain to his brain, rendering him immobile and useless on the wet earth, gritting his teeth until the pain began to wane, and ebbing and flowing like the tides of the sea. It took a herculean effort to sit upright and he began rubbing his muscles to get the circulation back.

The noise from the traffic on the ring road, which whizzed relentlessly around the small park, seemed deafening driving into his head like the pneumatic drills on the road works. The traffic exhaust fumes that hung in the air were choking.

Danny reached into his sock, took out his pink inhaler, shook it, and tried to take a puff. But to his dismay, it had run out of spray. Instead, he had to resort to coughing up heaps of phlegm.

Blackout.

Danny's brain snapped back into reality again from wherever he had left it and found himself still lying on the grass, but now he was surrounded by the usual suspects. The local hoi polloi of junkies and alcoholic reprobates. They were the roughest looking mob he had ever seen. They were all smashed out of their tiny minds even at this early hour, but truthfully, Danny didn't know if it was six o'clock at night or six in the morning, he had lost all track of time and was living in a permanent perpetual procession of blackouts.

Blackout.

Danny's mind snapped back again. He lay on the path, his face glued to the floor with vomit. The stench of stomach acid-filled Danny's nostrils and drooled into his brain as he painfully tore his stubbly cheeks from its adhesive grip. His hair spread and stuck to his face with sick.

The mob sat on the bench outside the old toilet block, slurping from special brew cans as car exhaust fumes dripped around them. Magda stood next to them, frozen like a statue in the park, her limbs fused and contorted at an impossible angle. Then she lurched and twisted her arms around the back of her head like an out of control robot, before collapsing to the ground in a twitching heap.

Thomas turned his radio up loud to drown out the arguing. Frank was snoring loudly inside his tent; he could sleep through an earthquake. Katrina was berating herself, screaming out crying then screaming some more. Martin was sleeping quietly in a semi-conscious stupor, and Harry was having the heebie-jeebies. Some nights he would lay in his tent screaming, hallucinating spiders were crawling all over him and giant wasps were buzzing around inside his tent.

Paulina appeared from nowhere, stomping towards the people around the fire, and started screaming at Thomas to turn the radio off. He wouldn't. The argument was escalating beyond control they were exchanging insults. Nose to nose spittle was flying. Paulina threw a hard punch. Thomas staggered back and fell on to his tent. Paulina turned off the radio and started crying, so did Thomas.

Elena ran over, grabbed Paulina by the hair, and started struggling with her they fell to the ground. Elena was spitting and scratching and biting like a wild animal. John tried to pull them apart. Pavel stood to the edge of the brawl and began jabbing the air with his fists, making punching sounds as he shimmied and ducked and weaved waving his head about, punching the air in front of him and throwing left and right hooks and uppercuts, clearly enjoying the fight.

John managed to drag them apart. Pavel stopped punching the air and just looked around in wind blurred confusion. Paulina went back inside her tent and started crying, wailing relentlessly with the rage and despair of a tortured soul rising along with the other shouting screaming, and oblivious noise making. Pavel went back inside his tent and covered himself in blankets, attempting to melt the chilliness of the air. His body dripping with confusion under the covers he soon calmed. Paulina and Thomas' sobbing started to grow weaker, but Katrina wouldn't stop wailing as she stood outside Harry's tent shuddering.

The toilets in the park were a well-known meeting place for sad old men who had to resort to meeting cheap prostitutes, young men, or sometimes boys, for illicit sex and drug dealing. Danny felt breathless. He reached inside his pocket to take out his pink inhaler just in case it would work this time. As he took it out from his pocket the twenty-pound note inside dropped to the floor. Danny quickly went to pick it up but not quickly enough.

Adolf rose to his feet and strode towards Danny. His psychotic glare, unwavering, fixed him in the eyes as he put his massive hands like shovels around his neck and started to squeeze. Nausea crept against Danny's lungs, adrenalin drooling again into his brain as he struggled to break free from his iron grip.

Adolf felt enormous power grow within him. Power of control. Danny couldn't speak, his voice had been taken from him. Fear rose in Danny's body as Adolf increased the pressure around Danny's throat, choking him of breath. Danny felt his heart press against his ribcage and his heart pumping in his ears. He reached out blindly gasping as he stole his final breaths. Danny's whole body became numb and useless. He could feel himself floating away from this life.

Adolf loosened his grip. Danny gasped for oxygen. Backing up against the wall, his helpless and alone face became white with terror as he crashed onto the prostitutes on the bench who quickly pushed him away. Adolf's fist smashed into Danny's face, knocking him to the ground and banging his head against the cracked concrete path. Adolf crouched over him trying to prise the twenty-pound note from his hand, but Danny wouldn't let go.

Adolf's rotten teeth sank into Danny's neck like Dracula letting the Twenty fall loose. Danny curled up into a tight ball and rolled on top of the money. He was lying on the ground groaning when the money came to the attention of one of the Slovaks. Slavomir was small, but he was like an angry Pitbull.

Danny gasped for oxygen, squirming underneath them like a slug as they rained down heavy blows onto his stricken body. Stamping, punching, and kicking. Danny was in no position or condition to fight back.

Adolf stood over him aiming kicks to his ribs, he then turned suddenly as Elena kicked him between the legs. Danny grabbed the money rolled along the ground past them, knocking into glass bottles on the path in the frenzy. Adolf pulled a knife and swiped at Danny, cutting his jacket missing his skin by millimetres. He tried again. Danny picked up a bottle and bought it down hard upon Adolf's head. Adolf dropped to his knees, blood pouring from his wound. Danny sent another bottle smashing down once more, Adolf's skull cracked splattering blood over Danny's face. Adolf just keeled over holding his head, blood seeping through his fingers.

Everyone dumbstruck, listening to Adolf's screams. His hands, jacket sleeves, and shoulders now soaked red and dripping with blood as it oozed out of his skull and poured down his body, dripping onto his shoes and the grass. Adolf, unsteady on his feet, began staggering around in circles.

Everyone backed away. Danny was the only one left on the bench as he slumped towards him and wavered in front of him, slashing his knife around, relishing the fear in everyone's eyes.

Danny wanted to grab the knife, but he was afraid of getting stabbed or catching AIDS. Adolf started staggering around in circles again, he didn't know where he was or where he was going. He then started to head towards the traffic.

Cars breaking and narrowly avoiding him. Adolf went weaving along the road, dripping blood. He seemed oblivious to the chaos he was causing. The long queue of traffic stuck behind him, sounding horns and drivers swearing at him as he staggered along the main road holding on to the knife.

A white van man saw something come out through the mist; a blurring image which slowly cleared to reveal itself. He gasped in sheer terror as he saw a blood-soaked knifeman heading straight into his path and started madly scrabbling with the controls. He swerved, mounted the kerb, and drove along with two wheels on and two off for ten meters until he eventually came to a screeching halt right in front of him. He watched blood smear across his windscreen as Adolf slid over his bonnet and rolled onto the ground.

3

'You're not supposed to drink any water,' the A&E nurse said, struggling to contain her anger and increasing stress, which were close to breaking point.

'Bollocks!' said Magda.

'Pardon?'

'Kurwa spierdolic!' She screwed up her face as she blasted the Polish nurse with her foul breath.

'You're sick, Magda. You need help, you are going to die if you carry on like this.'

'Maybe better for me dead,' Magda screamed, sweating and shaking to pieces, her eyes bloodshot full of terror and desperation.

'Think about your family, you can't die.'

'My family dead.'

'They're not dead they are-'

'You know nothing about my person. I better off dead,' she cut the nurse off, slurring and unable to focus.

'You don't mean that.'

'Smoke, tobacco please.'

'You can't you're in a hospital, Magda, you're sick.'

'Please, smoke.' Magda shifted around in her bed and tried pulling the saline drip from her arm. 'Smoke!'

'No!' the nurse shouted, trying to restrain her from removing the drip and holding her arms away.

'Why not!'

'You are in hospital, it's not allowed.'

'go outside.'

'Wait here.'

The student nurse left the cubicle and hot-footed it to the nursing station down the corridor. Doctors and nurses were all flying about in their starched white coats and blue uniforms, rushing in and out of cubicles whilst carrying bandages, clipboards, and bits of foam. In the corridor, a woman with a pair of crutches standing next to the wall crashed backwards. Her two friends noticing ran over, one of them put their coat under her head and they both put her in the recovery position. They looked up at the nurse as she came hurtling down the corridor towards them, then came skidding to a halt.

'Aren't you going to call someone?' they asked, condescendingly.

'I'm very sorry but I can't really I'm...'

Dazed and confused, the woman on the floor muttered in a weak and feeble voice as she gazed upon them in a trance. Her friends glaring at the nurse as if their friend was going to die.

'Have you got any medication or insulin?' the nurse asked as the woman began to bang her head against the floor, making facial contortions and started foaming at the mouth. Her body, hands, and head all together in a ceaseless flailing frenzy. The doctor began yelling at the nurse to get some insulin, as the woman shook violently on the floor and a colleague placed a blanket over her shaking limbs.

Outside the nursing station, a man was screaming his lungs

out. 'I'm not the fucking Easter bunny, I'm not Jesus Christ. Is this the death of humanity? Cease your Islamic, immoral, judgemental, Rasputin black magic and evil ideology!'

Reaching the nursing station, she explained what Magda was doing, collected some insulin and two nurses ran back up the blue line past the ranting man and saw the woman fitting on the floor. She gave the insulin to the Doctor and ran back to Magda.

Further down the ward. Every fibre of Danny's being was screaming for mercy, begging for forgiveness. He sobbed barely able to speak, gasping for breath, and shaking apart.

Perspiration was seeping from every pore only he was frozen to the core. Jolts charged through his poisoned body as he lay cowering on his hospital bed. Fear gripped him as the voices in his head grew louder.

'No, you can't smoke, you are very ill. If you smoke you will be even worse,' said the staff nurse.

'I know my body, not your body!'

'No! Magda, put back the drip.' Both nurses started grappling with her and managed to put the drip back into her arm.

Magda went calm for a few minutes and the senior nurse left. The other nurse sat down on the bed with Magda and held her hand, exasperated.

Delirium descended upon Danny, slowly covering him like a sheet. His whole soul felt consumed by the demonic force. Dark shadows loomed the feeling poured over him, like a great wave swallowing him deeper into the black abyss. Dark shadowy figures pushed themselves through the walls from hell to claim his soul. Blinding flashes and wailing voices of the damned. Satan's mocking sounds trapped inside his fevered mind, unable to be set free, echoing around him and dragging his wretched soul deeper down.

Evil descending, thrashing and weeping. Dark shadows are creeping. His body now weakening. The devil is reaping.

Danny saw a woman approaching. Her eyes were burning, and two small horns protruded from her head. Danny felt a sharp pain in his side. Blackout.

'Please you get me spice?'

'Spice! No, you can't smoke that either.'

'Shhh. You never listen. You no understand. Please you give me money for a taxi?'

'You can't leave.'

'Why not?'

'You are sick.'

'I no sick I want go home.'

Magda started pulling at the drip again. The student nurse ran back down the corridor in the direction of the nursing station. A couple of paramedics burst through a side door almost colliding with her, pushing someone in a wheelchair who was coughing up blood into a plastic bowl. They bolted past her and smashed through a set of double doors. Outside the nursing station, the man was still ranting in the grip of a psychotic episode.

'You are agents. Secret agents working for North Korea, China and Mongolia,' he paused for a moment. 'All the might of Asia will descend upon us and we shall all be eating monkey brains for breakfast!'

Lying on the corridor floor the woman on crutches was still in the throes of an epileptic seizure. As the student nurse approached the nursing station, she stopped to help. Bright lights, noise commotion and chaos. The young nurse on the job didn't know where she was.

'OK, one, two, three, and lift!' The two nurses and doctor lifted her from the floor to the bed.

'I'm dying,' She mumbled, or so she thought.

'You're not dying,' the nurse told her.

'Yes, I am.'

'Do you know your name?'

'No.'

'OK, do you know where you are?' the doctor asked as the nurse wrapped a pressure gauge around her arm which she then inflated.

'Blood pressure increasing one-eighty over eighty,' the nurse then went to check her pulse.

'Don't let me die,' she managed to mumble as she twisted her head around her body, shaking on the bed wrapped up like a kipper in a giant foil bag, watching concerned faces peering down at her and ceiling strobe lights passing over her head as she was being wheeled down the blue line.

'Pulse one-thirty.'

'Where am I?' she slurred.

The Doctor shone a bright light into her eyes. She flinched. She panted; her breathing was laboured. She felt as if her heart was going to pack up on her.

The patient groaned and thrashed about trying to lift herself, but she couldn't. Her moans echoed down the corridor as she threw up all over the young nurse. Two porters took over as the nurses had to rush away.

Danny's brain kept snapping back into reality with each returning ray of consciousness from wherever he had left it.

Suspicious of his surroundings, and still afraid of what horrors may be lurking, he slowly tried opening his eyes. The satanic forces that had invaded the darker crevasses of his mind seemed to have faded to nothing. Into focus, there came a plastic tube inserted into his arm which was connected to a clear bottle of fluid, strapped to a long metal pole. Recognising this as a saline drip, he realised that he must be in a hospital. He felt as if an elephant had been using his head like a football and dancing the can-can on his chest. As he opened his eyes the room came into focus. Every ounce of his flesh felt dull with pain. Danny could hear the argument from his bed escalating.

Magda struggled with the nurses, but she pulled out the drip from her arm. Blood trickled down her wrist and she held it up laughing. The student nurse felt the blood drain from her face as it drained from her arm. Magda started screaming and the student nurse broke from the pressure and began to cry.

'I want go home, I not stay here,' yelled Magda. The student felt the same way.

The senior nurse turned to the student. 'Sorry, but I need you to leave,' she pressed the panic button. Two more nurses came in and pulled the curtains around the bed. All you could hear was a barrage of foul language, screaming obscenities, and then silence. Ten seconds later they came out.

'Sorry, we had to sedate her. She's a danger to herself.' They looked red-faced and exhausted.

'Go and clean yourself up immediately you're covered, it is unhygienic,' she told the young nurse.

'I know I'm sorry,' she said, just holding it together.

Danny lifted his weary head from the pillow, screwing up his eyes against the light in pain. He had no idea how he got here. A quiet voice aroused him from his lethargy. Someone was sitting at the edge of the bed and the other side of the curtain had been pulled to separate him from the other patient.

'How are you feeling?'

'Lousy.' Danny recognised the voice of the old sergeant.

'Do you remember what happened?'

'I fell down some steps.'

'Did you recognise who did this to you?'

Dazed and confused, five minutes passed without a reply as Danny just stared blankly at the wall. His head felt separate from his body and he thought he would never get the two back together again.

'Are you alright, Danny?'

'I suppose I must be in some kind of shock or something.'

'Very likely.'

'I'm, I'm, I'm,' Danny tried to mouth the words but all he could do was stammer and choke on them. Tears welled up in his eyes.

'Try to get a grip?'

'I'm disgusting,' he blubbered.

'Different, but not disgusting.'

'I'm sick,' things started going through Danny's mind, thoughts that scared him and made him feel that he had to escape. Danny didn't even want to think about what happened. In fact, he told himself that he would never think about what happened ever again. He would bury the memory deep inside himself and hope it would never see the light of day. Danny vowed he would take this secret to the grave and hoped nobody would ever find out. But he couldn't escape them. 'I hate myself I wish I was dead.'

'You hear about people who die all the time in this job. Young kids leaving their poor families behind, heartbroken. It's not fair and it's no joke. I wish I could detach myself from it all, but you can't. You should never say things like that.'

'You don't care.'

'Of course, I care. If I didn't, I wouldn't be here now. I was the sod that found you... is there anyone I can call for you?'

'I have no one.'

'Parents?'

Painful thoughts stirred in Danny's dim and distant memory. Memories he had repressed for a long time began to resurface again.

'Danny?'

'They got killed you know, my parents. Car accident. I was adopted, but it's the same thing. I never knew my real mum and dad. My real mum got rid of me, didn't want to know. All I know was that she was Lithuanian, don't even have a name. I think she was a drug addict. That's probably where I get it from.'

'When's your birthday Danny?'

'Why,' he laughed. 'You gonna buy me a present?'

'Danny, when is your birthday?'

'I was born on Christmas day, 1995, St Thomas's, at Four o'clock in the morning.'

Tony felt like his heart had exploded in his chest, leaving him shaken to the core. He just stared at Danny in disbelief. He drew long, slow, deep breaths, and tried to calm himself down. Tony sat back in his chair, clutching his heart tearfully. He knew something Danny didn't.

'Am I in trouble? Am I gonna go to prison?'

'I don't think so… self-defence.'

'Adolf dead?'

'No, unfortunately.'

'I'm tired of this.'

'Maybe we can help.'

'How?'

'Information. You help us, we help you.'

4

SEVEN MONTHS LATER.

Danny fished half a mars bar out of his coat pocket and held it out to the fox's gaping jaws. The fox snapped the chocolate from his hand, its slimy tongue tickling his fingers.

Danny could hear a distant blues guitar rhythm, blasting the waking hours, as he trudged up the hill in the direction of the subway.

At the entrance to the subway stood a man, rubbish blowing around his feet as he continued strumming his guitar. The music tugged at Danny's soul, but amidst those subterranean blues that echoed down that dark passageway, more of societies unfortunates slept and sheltered, tugging around inside their sleeping bags, looking for some recognition, some kindly attitude from the passing crowd. They didn't get any.

The day was breaking as Danny began to reach the end of the tunnel, the music still floating down with him and the volume slowly drifting in and out with the futility of existence flaying around him. He emerged already at this early hour to the sweet and sickly aroma of marijuana hung in the air.

That morning, Magda was standing by the clock tower hassling people for money near the cash point. She was agitated. She always dressed smartly. You could pick up some classy outfits from the salvation army for a pound, so she said.

And every day she looked different. She had dyed her hair from blonde to red, and she carried on harassing people for money. She spotted Danny coming around the corner, wheeling his blue bin trolley.

'Danny,' she shouted. You always heard her before you saw her. She rushed over to him and pulled him close.

'Danny, please, money for a cup of coffee?'

'No. No more.'

'Why not?' her face flashed rage for an instant.

'I have none.'

'Bullshit! Please, just five pounds for coffee?'

'Coffee is one pound.'

'Huh, you're not my friend. I thought you had a good heart… bullshit.'

'I won't give you money for drugs.'

'No drugs… just coffee.'

'You lie.'

'You know me, no liar bollocks,' she stomped off in the direction of Mc Donald's and started hassling people outside. It wouldn't take her long to get the money.

It was bitterly cold and there wasn't much shelter to be found. The Christmas market was up and running, and there was a long line of wooden sheds. Concessions selling Christmas fair items and tasty food. A busker was playing what looked like alpine cowbells. It created a hypnotic sound and summoned up the image of cold arctic wind, blowing across the tundra and over a herd of a thousand reindeers. It got earlier every year.

Danny recognised a couple of familiar faces in the crowds. Prolific shoplifters with long coats and long pockets. They had already been spotted by security and they were being monitored. It was always the same ones. Danny knew Magda used to shoplift and that she had slept on the blue mattress a few times but thought she didn't do it anymore. But Magda could make more money far more easily by using her feminine charms. Flirting and cosying up to lonely old men who would give her half their pension money for some much-needed attractive female attention and companionship. There wasn't many of them left that she hadn't got her claws into.

Danny heard someone behind him. He turned sharply in the direction of the voice. The old man's face was weather-beaten and ruddy with sore squinting eyes. His thick Latvian accent was practically incomprehensible, and he was obviously drunk, judging by his opinions and wild manner. Danny greeted him.

'Bastards just look at these bastards,' Danny turned to look at the shoppers. 'Oh, look at me,' Pavel said, shaking his hips. 'I go to the town shopping; I buy a shirt two hundred pounds from Fenwick... I hate these bastards... oh look at me!' He then looked back at Danny pathetically, 'please you have just one pound for coffee, please sir, I have no money.'

Danny reached into his back pocket and gave him a pound.

'God bless you,' Pavel said as he staggered off.

Early this morning the pavements had been strewn with litter, debris, puddles of vomit, puddles of piss, and broken glass. But you would never know it.

As Danny pushed his trolley further along the road, he could not tell what it was at first. It looked more like a wild animal than a human being. A grubby twisted creature hunched over, searching through the rubbish bins and poking around the ashtrays for dog ends.

As Danny walked past, he offered her a cigarette. Danny

didn't smoke himself, but he often found packets with some left in them and kept them for people. Danny offered her one.

'Please take one,' Danny said.

'It speaks.'

'Sorry?'

'I'm surprised you have the intelligence to speak, sweeping up shit for a living,' she growled.

'It's a job.'

'Don't talk to me, scum!'

Danny could tell she was from the local mental hospital it was only half a mile away and the town was full of the unfortunates.

'Sorry,' Danny said, as she glared at him in a mentally disturbed manner.

As Danny turned and walked along the colonnade in front of the bus lanes, the path became dirtier. Broken glass, milkshake, fast food wrappers, and over-flowing bins. There was a group of people huddled together on some steps, they were singing and pushing each other around to the sound of an old radio. They didn't care how they sang or screamed, as long as they didn't have to listen to the thoughts in their heads.

Further along, Cam sat in his usual spot with his placard which read: 'no muny for fud pleez help happy Crismas.' He had been using it for six months now.

Cam had been on the streets for four years, but he was only twenty years old. He always sat reading a book, yet he couldn't actually read. He had severe dyslexia. Some people didn't like to talk about how they wound up on the street, it was just easier that way.

'Ok boss,' said Cam.

'Seen Magda?' Danny asked.

'Yes.'

'What's wrong with her?'

'She's schizo.'

'What?'

'Bipolar or borderline personality disorder, one or the other. Nuts basically.'

'No, seriously, what do you thinks wrong with her?'

'The drugs have fucked her brain up, Danny, She's psychotic dude. It kills your brain cells.'

'Will she get better?'

'Yeah, maybe two years in rehab.'

Danny gave him a cigarette out of his pocket. Cam lit it and took a puff. 'She's using you dude,' he continued. 'She uses everyone she's figured out a way of doing it and she's good at it… makes everyone feel sorry for her all the time. You can't help her, she just wants your money. She doesn't give a fuck about anyone except herself… She's just mugging you off… She's a manipulative sociopath if you want the truth. You can't help her, so stop trying. It's too late.'

'It's never too late,' said Danny.

Cam creased up in a wheezing chuckle.

'Look you seem like a decent person, wouldn't want to see you get hurt. Keep away from her, she's bad news.' Cam looked at Danny and smiled broadly exposing his decaying drug addict teeth. 'You know it anyway,' he said.

'No,' replied Danny.

'You're thinking it anyway. When is she happiest, with you?'

Danny said nothing.

'When you're giving her money.'

Danny wondered if he was wasting his time and wondered if it was worth trying. Everyone told him to stay away from her. They all said that she would destroy him; cut his throat and stab him in the back. But Danny wouldn't give up on her, even if everybody else had.

'Danny!' Magda bounded up to Danny, put her arms around him and gave him a big wet kiss on the cheek. Then she put her bag on top of the bin took out some apples, tangerines and a carton of drink and shoved them into Danny's pockets.

'Eat, good for you. What time you finish work?'

'Seven I think.'

'Everybody kiss my arse,' she said.

'Well, you do have a good arse,' replied Danny. She laughed.

'Go Manchester tomorrow, watch football?' she asked. Cam shook his head. 'Maybe you come?'

'Busy,' said Danny.

'Always busy …. King Harry give me one million pounds next week, maybe two.'

'Have you taken anything,' Danny asked.

'Just beer, you want to try?' Magda unzipped her bag and gave Danny a can of Tyskie.

'I'm in AA remember, cannot drink.'

Cam smirked. Magda looked in her bag and took out a packet of Polish pastries.

'For you, eat.'

'No, you have.'

'No, not me, you. I not hungry, go eat.' Danny took her food. His pockets were stuffed full of her food.

'America drop bombs on Afghanistan, two thousand children, dead, why?'

'Don't know.'

'Terribow. This man never has sex with a woman, tiny dick.' She told Cam, who collapsed with a fit of the giggles, his eyes were watering so much he had to take his glasses off.

'Thanks,' said Danny.

'Why your beautiful face,' she touched Danny's face as to brush away a hair on his cheek, 'come walk with me.'

They left Cam and walked together through the crowds. She stopped to pick up an empty fast-food wrapper and put it into one of the bin liners in his trolly.

'I help you, what time you finish?'

'Seven-thirty.'

'You want coffee, I get you coffee. Magda no liar.'

'OK.'

'Yury punch me.'

'No.'

'Yes, look,' Magda lifted up her hair and jumper revealing her stomach but Danny saw no bruises. 'Yury too much heroin.'

'No.'

'Yes, Yury alcoholic.'

'Well, maybe.'

Danny liked Yury. Yes, he drank and got himself into a few punch ups. He was Russian. Drinking and fighting were just what he did. He never touched smack. Danny thought.

They trudged determinedly, weaving their way through the impossible movement of human traffic. Danny pushing his blue trolly of bin bags through the shopping centre with his friend beside him. The noise echoing around them was disorientating. It was difficult navigating their way through the hordes.

All life was here. Disabled, mad, drunk, homeless, and drug-addled people, rubbing along with the shoppers on a busy Wednesday afternoon.

Danny stopped at another bin. Unlocked it, took out the liner, replaced it, and gave it a spray and wipe. Magda often followed him around at work. His work colleagues were used to it. It amused them.

'I have terribow headache,' she moaned.

'You drink too much.'

'I stop everything next week, drink, cigarettes, marijuana. I promise I get job in packhouse. I good picker. Five hundred pounds a week.'

'No way.'

'Yes, Lomax fruits give me a contract.' She cuddled up to Danny and took his hand, 'why you no girlfriend? Your beautiful face. Maybe me your girlfriend, maybe we marry?'

'What about Yury?'

'He doesn't matter to my person.'

'What about Max?'

'Max dickhead too much, speak blah blah blah. Too much detective. You stay with me and I look after you. Maybe you father for Joseph, maybe Yury go prison.'

'Maybe.'

Yury did go to prison quite a lot.

They passed Gerry who was burning the chewing gum off the pavement. He had what looked like a giant vacuum cleaner strapped to his back and it worked by pumping highly corrosive chemicals down through a long hose and out through the nozzle which melted the gum. He looked just like one of the Ghostbusters.

'They should issue us with taser guns, we could taser the bastards when they spit it out,' Gerry said.

Just then a red balloon gently floated in his direction. He stamped on it so hard it sounded like a bomb going off. The sound of vibrating bounced off all the buildings. Everybody suddenly froze for a few seconds.

A baby started crying. Gerry looked around innocently. A child was struggling to push her disabled mother up a steep incline, a man whose body was so disfigured it was hard to look at, and a blonde woman crying, were among the continuous stream of people flowing like a great river through a gorge of stores.

'You know I love your person,' Magda said, stroking her hand on Danny's chest and squeezing his arm, 'you give me everything I will pay back I promise one day you come to my home I cook for you.'

'When?'

'You stay with me next Merry Christmas in beautiful home, I help you I promise.'

'Maybe.'

'Danny, please, money for tobacco? I stop two weeks, I promise.'

'Two weeks...ok,' Danny reached into his pocket and gave her ten pounds. Magda kissed him on the cheek and ran off through the precinct stopping suddenly to kiss a small child on the head.

'See you later baby!' she screamed out then disappeared.

5

'What Annunaki reptiles,' Danny asked.

'Annunaki race,' he blabbered on in his incredible broad Brummie accent. 'Blood drinking, flesh-eating, shape-shifting, extra-terrestrials who want to take over the planet. They have controlled us since the dawn of time. The queen and all the world leaders are Annunaki sons of Anu.'

'Who's Anu?'

'Annunaki are the sons of Anu who came from a distant galaxy.'

'OK.'

'The Annunaki ruled the Iggi until the Iggi died and then they created us in their place.'

He just appeared from nowhere out of the crowd dressed head to foot in his bright yellow reflector clothes and an Australian hat with his little dog yapping beside him. Glaring at Danny with his yellow eyes and yellow teeth to match his clothes.

'I don't understand,' Danny said.

'The Annunaki are a race of beings that travelled across the depths of space and time until they reached earth. They ruled the Iggi who lived on the planet before we did and then they created mankind.'

'Where did they come from?'

'They came from the planet Nibiru, its twenty million light-years from earth.'

'So are you,' Danny thought, looking down at his shoes that were coming away from the sole. 'What size are you, ten? I found a nice pair of desert boots yesterday if you like I can bring them up the centre Friday?' Danny asked.

You would be amazed at what some people throw away. Danny was forever rescuing expensive new coats, trousers, shirts, jumpers, and shoes out of dustbins. He would collect them and keep them all together in bin liners at the back of one of their storage cupboards so if any of the homeless people needed a new pair of shoes a nice warm coat or anything else, they would come to him.

Danny was providing a much-needed service. Sometimes he would take them up to the homeless shelter. He knew all the street people personally and as he worked as a street cleaner now, he would come into daily contact with them all. Danny was still part of their world.

Fred cleared off. 'See you Friday, come on Suzi,' he shouted at his little dog, yanking the lead.

Tramping through the streets after work Danny was off to his meeting. It was six-thirty and the blues guitar rhythm floated down the high street. There were people in every doorway collecting change in cups and hats, slurping from cans or curled up in sleeping bags.

Danny saw Magda sitting in a shop doorway looking across at him.

'Hey, baby…where you go?'

'Meeting.'

'I walk with you.'

'Sure.'

Danny helped her up, she was wobbling a bit and he grabbed her arm. A gypsy woman jumped out in front of them holding a sprig of heather.

She began to speak, 'I can see —'

'No thank you very much,' said Magda, as she gripped Danny firmly and pushed him over to the other side of the road. Two kids on bicycles dressed in all black with scarfs around their mouths headed towards them and then circled them twice.

'Magda, Magda,' they called.

'Hey, baby.'

'You want anything?'

'Sorry baby, maybe later.'

They cycled away, kicking their front wheels up and wheeling nonchalantly through the crowd.

'Nice children,' Magda said. 'Buy Hamburger,' she said as they stood outside the Chicken Cottage.

They got their usual at the takeaway, double cheeseburger, coke, fries and chilli bites. 'Too much salad,' said Magda. Everybody was staring, as usual, but Danny ignored them.

It was warm inside, and Danny's clothes were sticking to him, so he decided to take off his coat. God, she looked beautiful, he thought to himself. Underneath Magda's coat, she was dressed in a tight-fitting bright yellow dress with too much flesh on show.

'You eat... just quick smoke,' she said and went outside.

It wasn't busy inside the restaurant, there were lots of empty tables and chairs. One lad with a pizza face was busy mopping the floor while he chatted to his female colleague who was busy clearing tables. He was complaining about the manager who wouldn't give him Saturday off to watch the football. She told him that football was a stupid game and that real men played rugby. He had to keep going over the floor again and again as people left dirty footprints on their way out.

Danny sat watching Magda through the glass door. Security at work would be watching her too. They were always watching them. Danny always had to take off his work jacket when he was with her, but he always forgot. Still, they amused security.

Magda opened the door. 'Five minutes,' she shouted.

One minute had passed and there she was, as usual, shouting at people across the street. 'Roman, Roman!' you could hear her scream as she rushed across the road to talk to people. Another user or dealer friend usually. She threw the fag butt, on the ground, and came back in.

'Eat,' she said. 'Roman five years army Afghanistan, his mother professor of Oxford University mathematics,' Magda said as she tucked into her burger, 'why you do not eat... tired?'

'Yes, tired.'

'Day off, go park together?'

A stranger sitting in the corner of the restaurant, minding his own business, caught her eye. 'This man FBI,' she said.

All Danny could do was let it fly over his head and let others snigger. Magda checked her phone for messages.

'Take That have come to town.'

She showed Danny photographs of the band Take That in a magazine. She claimed she knew Robbie Williams and that they once had a relationship.

'Not marry, just sex. Robbie good sex. I love Robbie Williams. Paparazzi shhh... Tony says FBI come to town next month. Tony tells me Russian mafia non-stop sell drugs to children. This is terribow, too much danger.'

'Take That is coming?'

'Yes.'

'No.'

'It's true, you know me no liar.'

Magda got out her bag and searched through her make-up and documents from probation and social services mental health. 'Shit, no money,' she looked at Danny seductively, 'Coca-Cola please very much. You give me money for marijuana?'

'No, you have to stop smoking that.'

'Please, baby,' she stroked Danny's arm.

'I don't like it when you smoke drugs.'

'You not my husband, you not tell me what to do!'

'I don't.'

'You do… oh, Magda, no smoke, no drink, it's bad for you,' she mimicked him.

'It is.'

'Heroin bad, marijuana good… no stress.'

'It makes it worse,' said Danny.

'No… you not my psychiatrist… too much speak, zip it.'

Danny gave in and gave her a tenner, 'no more food or drugs your choice.'

Magda took the money and kissed Danny on top of the head, then ran outside for another smoke. The radio was playing in the restaurant, it was the eight o'clock news bulletin. The main headline was about a man who got stabbed to death by his mentally ill girlfriend.

The thirty-year-old man was murdered by his

twenty-eight-year-old girlfriend during a psychotic episode. She had a chronic addiction to marijuana and was suffering from bipolar disorder. Later on, they had an interview with a politician who blamed the government for cutting support to mental health patients.

Suddenly, a man staggered through the door under the weight of his heavy rucksack. Magda stood in the doorway shouting at him., 'Ahhh! No more bomb, this man terrorist!'

Everyone stood and stared. Danny just ignored her. Then like a flick of a switch, Magda was calm again. Danny just sat there drinking his Coca-Cola, thinking about that woman who stabbed her boyfriend.

'Buy chicken bargain bucket, twelve pieces chicken for nine ninety-nine. Mm, I wait for more food.'

Danny went up to the counter. Through the window, he could see her having an animated conversation with someone. It was friendly and non-hostile. Then she gave him a big hug and kiss. Danny made the order and waited to be served.

A few minutes later, a girl gave him the bucket of chicken and he went back outside to her.

'Magda,' a man sitting in a doorway shouted as he gulped down vodka.

'Hey, baby,' she replied. He beckoned her over and Danny waited as they chatted. 'Danny, please give me some chicken.'

Danny gave it, reluctantly. She then gave it to the man and kissed him, which annoyed Danny. They moved on further up the street which meant more people for Magda to bump into. It was a never-ending succession of hugging, kissing and giving out chicken. Danny felt like a mobile takeaway for the homeless. A man shuffled past them, blown out of his head on something.

'Heroin dickhead,' Magda screamed at him. The man ignored her. More down and outs shuffled by. Another endless stream of 'hey, baby, you alright?' or 'heroin dickhead!' and more chicken handouts.

They spotted the man down a narrow side street, lying on the pavement barefoot, drooling and shrouded in mist.

'Cam,' Magda shouted. No response. She stomped forwards angrily, 'Cam,' she shouted in his face as she knelt next to him and shoved him. 'Kurwa!' she continued. Cam just lay on the ground unmoving. 'Too much heroin,' Magda told Danny. 'Come on, baby, give me water.'

Danny took a bottle of water from inside his coat pocket and handed it to her. She lifted Cam's chin and tried to pour water into his mouth, but it just trickled out. She opened his mouth, tipped Cam's head back and tried again. She then poured some water over his head and smoothed it into his har like shampoo. 'Cam, this happens sometimes, don't worry,' she said.

The alleyway was deserted, but just around the corner was a busy pub with people blissfully unaware. You could hear them shouting and laughing on their night out with friends.

'Come on Cam!' Magda screamed, 'what is this, where are his parents, just a child Cam!'

Cam groaned, 'I know, baby, I know.'

Magda slapped his back hard. Cam groaned some more. A person walked past and said nothing. Magda pointed at half a bottle of Coca Cola discarded along the pavement.

'Coca Cola please,' said Magda. Danny got it for her. She repeated the exercise, holding his mouth open and pouring the drink down him. She wet his hair again with some more water.

'Come on Cam. Two minutes.' She told Danny.

'Urgh!' Cam spewed from his stomach, coughed and sputtered everywhere. His eyes opened.

'Magda,' Cam slurred.

'OK. Now everything alright,' she said, then slapped him hard on the back. 'I just save your life!'

Cam became more alert. He manoeuvred himself to an upright position, looked up and recognised Danny.

'OK, boss,' Cam chuckled.

'Cam, look, water and Coca Cola,' she put them down beside him. 'We go now.'

They left Cam.

Turning back to the old main drag, they ran into Marta. Marta was a young Polish girl from the local church. She was busy with her friends, handing out food parcels and pouring out hot tea from a flask. She did this every night. They said hello.

Marta started talking to Magda in Polish. Magda could speak a few different languages, but Danny wasn't sure exactly where Magda came from. Marta offered Danny some hot tea from her flask. Danny reminded her that he wasn't homeless anymore. She said that it didn't matter.

Marta went over to the other side of the street to the man who slept under the white duvet outside the Super Drug store. He was a new arrival and he had half his ears chopped off. Most people didn't talk to him and he was alienated from the homeless community. The police wanted him to leave town and for good reason.

Marta was sat on the wall next to him and they were talking. When Magda saw this, she went ballistic. Magda started shouting and screaming at Marta in her native tongue. Marta just stood there and took it. Danny grabbed Magda by the shoulders and told her to calm down.

'No, no give this man food. This man sex with children five-six years, this man-monster!' Steve, the child rapist, enjoyed seeing Magda angry. 'I know what you do,' Magda continued, 'you not wanted here, go leave I kill you I swear!'

'OK, if this is the case, but he is still a person who is hungry, he needs food,' said Marta.

'I can't believe this you know what this is Marta. You have sister six years you like this man have sex with your sister?' shouted Magda.

Marta looked shocked. They stared at each other like a couple of gunfighters in the old west.

'Why this man not prison, why this man not dead. You give me gun and I kill this person I promise.'

Steve just stayed under the covers enjoying the argument, whilst they were drawing attention to themselves.

'I kill you Russian mafia,' Magda said, imitating shooting him with a gun. Danny looked around nervously. He was still in his work clothes and security would be watching him right now.

Danny remembered the day he walked into the centre and saw that strange new man with half his ears chopped off. Fifty per cent of the rough sleepers had spent time inside at one point or another, so they knew the signs. They figured it out.

Danny remembered the night they decided to approach him about it. A few of them were sitting on the steps outside the Super Drug store. They just asked him flat out, 'are you a paedophile?' He was very matter of fact about it. He had no shame, felt no guilt or remorse. He told them all the gory details revelled in his notoriety. I will spare you.

One girl, one boy, five and six years old. He never moved from the view of the CCTV. He knew his life was at risk. He came down this way after being badly beaten up in Glasgow. Danny told the police about him as they didn't know. He told them that he wished he didn't know all these dangerous people. The police told Danny they were glad he did. Danny knew a lot of things they didn't. He was a useful source of information when necessary.

Security followed Steve with the cameras constantly. They even had two guards on twenty-four-hour Steve watch. They even followed him into the public lavatories when he took a slash. Steve quite enjoyed his notoriety in a sick and twisted kind of way.

'Come on, Magda, don't talk to him. He's a bad person, come on,' Danny grabbed her and moved her on. They passed Trudy on a bicycle, she looked awful. She was pale, stick thin, and she had lesions on her once beautiful face. It sent shivers down Danny's spine. Magda kissed her.

'Hi baby,' said Trudy, then she cycled on.

'What's wrong, your face gone white?' Magda shouted.

'Did you see her face, what's wrong with her?' replied Danny.

'Drugs, heroin, maybe infection,' said Magda.

'Aids.'

'Maybe life, just life.'

6

There can't be many things more degrading in life than being pissed on while you are asleep, but that's how Danny woke up. Two shadows were looming over him and the hot pungent aroma of a golden shower street style, but by the time Danny had struggled up out of his sleep coma they had scampered down the cobbled street.

Danny couldn't feel his hands. His fingers had fused and the yellow liquid on his sleeping bag had frosted up in a matter of seconds. It was minus five degrees and he was under the arches of a parade of shops. Someone was snoring next to him; the dawn chorus was in full swing. Danny hadn't died although he felt like death. It felt like his head was being squeezed in a vice. He had no memory of the night before or how he got here. The people he was sleeping with were still alive.

Many people have died of hypothermia, living it rough on the streets. An old-timer once told him that it felt like pins and needles all over your body, as your core temperature drops your blood freezes inside your veins, your heart then slows and you can't move or talk. You die an agonising death if no one is there to rescue you in time.

You could get sleeping bags that were insulated for up to minus thirty, in theory, but it was hard to stay warm. Heroin was probably the only solution to staying warm for some, but in reality, it acted only as a psychological barrier against the cold and you could still die of hypothermia.

Danny didn't have to sleep on the streets anymore, he did it by choice. Sargent Tony had pulled a few strings and got him into a halfway house. He had also managed to secure him a job with the council, but bad habits were hard to break, and he had to return the favour.

Danny picked up his aching limbs and headed in the direction of the town. Along that wind-blown street a million shopping bags, fast food wrappers, and cartons washed over the cobbles and towards Danny like a great plastic tidal surge.

Further down on the bridge, an old man in a three-piece suit sat in the road and stared down the pavement and through the deluge of flying debris at Danny, who was heading in his direction.

Danny saw a crushed-up man with a crushed-up beer can in his hand, sitting on a cracked pavement slab like a rubbish magnet. He didn't seem to know or care as all manner of filth piled up over his body and hit him in the face. All he said was, 'fuck you all,' screaming to all and sundry on a Sunday morn.

Danny walked over to him and grabbed hold of the black iron railing with his shaking hands, he then poked his head through as if looking through prison bars and down to the cold grey waters rippling in the misty morning light and watched driftwood gently floating under the bridge.

Alexander Strauss, address not fixed, spent his whole day wandering around the city with his two bags for life, poking through the ashtrays on top of the bins looking for 'doggies' half-decent dog ends. His pockets were fit to bursting point.

Danny offered him a new cigarette he examined it.

'No like.'

'Why not?'

'These taste better,' he said, showing him the lipstick-stained cigarettes in his pockets.

'How about I find you a nice Havana, so long,' he demonstrated with his fingers apart and pretended to puff on the imaginary cigar. 'Like Winston Churchill,' he continued.

'Ok,' Danny replied, and they shook hands.

'See you later my friend,' he said whilst rooting through another bin.

Moving past Wilko, Rupert was sitting on his favourite bench, clutching his heart and wheezing loudly.

'Help me, help me, please,' he called out. Most people ignored him. A few people stopped to see if he was alright but then moved on swiftly. As Danny got closer, an attractive woman asked Rupert if he was alright.

'Please, please help me.'

'What's the matter, is it your heart? Do you want me to call someone maybe an ambulance or a security guard?

'Please sit down next to me, I just want to talk to you.'

'I'm busy I'm on my lunch break,' the woman replied, 'do you need help?'

'Please sit down and talk to me. I'm so lonely, I just want a friend. Please can you be my friend?'

She looked flustered, 'sorry I can't help you I'm busy,' she moved on quickly.

'Please I'm so lonely,' he shouted, then went back to clutching his heart and wheezing.

Rupert wasn't homeless, really, and you couldn't even accuse him of doing anything bad. He had a nice room in sheltered accommodation, but he spent all day sitting on that bench. He didn't really have a bad heart; he was in good physical health, but he did look a bit unusual. He was a big man with a huge curly mop of black hair and wore glasses with incredible thick lenses so when you were close up to him his eyes looked enormous.

Past Pavarotti's on the corner, Danny past the blind man and his lover, they were both homeless and weighed down with heavy rucksacks, struggling to get through the impatient hordes. Behind them was Brian, a.k.a. catalogue man, who wandered around posing and pointing like a man out of a fashion magazine. They pumped fists.

Further along, a man sat against the wall muttering audible nonsense to himself.

'People ask me that question all the time, they're getting nothing out of me, nothing is real it's just a dream. All these people they don't exist they're just holograms, illusions, the whole worlds just made out of plasticine. Everybody is out to get you. Don't trust anyone, it's all lies, all lying bastards everyone one of them. I could tell them how it's gonna be, but it would be too much for em. They couldn't take it they think they know me, but they don't know me. The clock is ticking tick tock tick tock tick tock,' he went on.

'He's right you know,' a sarcastic shopper told Danny.

Outside Primark, Rory was strumming his guitar he couldn't play, and he couldn't sing, but in his mind, he was Bob Dylan. He started singing again and it was grating. A local thug walked past with his giggling girlfriend and a vicious looking Pitbull. He drank from a bottle of vodka. They gave him a dirty look, laughed and moved on.

Rory wound up on the streets after a relationship break-down, so many do. She wanted him out and her new fella in. It was her flat. She didn't care what he did or where he went. The sad thing was he still loved her and wrote songs about her. Sometimes he would be singing a well-known love song by another singer like the country and western song Joleen, but he would change the name to hers. 'Pauline, Pauline, Pauline, Pau-line.' It was very sad.

Further down, Danny saw Pavel hobbling towards him on a pair of crutches and a bandage around his head.

'Look at me! I all fucked up.'

'How did you wind up on those things?'

'I fuck myself up so much on drink. I drink myself legless ha. Doctor says bad blood if I no stop drink, I be dead two years.' He screamed whilst he searched around his coat pocket, took out half a bottle of scotch, unscrewed the cap and gulped the rest down.

'So why?' said Danny.

'So why I no stop. What would you do if you told you only two years live, I get drunk as fast as possible?'

Danny spotted sister Josephine walking towards them. She was a nun from the blessed virgin church and she worked as a volunteer down at the project. She knew them both. Danny often chatted to her or played the odd game of connect four with her. She offered her hand for him to shake. She was loud and in her black robes which flapped in the breeze. Danny's soul always seemed to melt in her gaze.

With his eyes cast down at her shoes and slowly examining the rest of her body, Danny knew what Pavel was thinking. He gave him a knowing look and motioned to the nun. She oozed sex appeal if that were possible for a nun.

'Ah ma poor son I see you are afflicted with the most terrible burden you should come to pray with me… it is said that upon the sight of God, men and women have thrown away their sticks and have walked again,' she said in her booming Nigerian accent.

'Bullshit, I never get my fucking legs fixed. It's a lot of bullshit crazy nun.'

'It's OK, I understand your anger and pain,' she replied.

'God won't help me. Argh, crazy nun go back to Africa!'

'Oh, don't talk such nonsense, my child, for God will see fit in his powers unknown to you to help you walk again.'

'What powers?' Pavel asked.

'His powers, his infinite divine powers you shall bear witness to the miracle of his healing.'

'Bah crazy nun!'

'I must go, bless you, my child,' she went, and Pavel watched her holy arse wiggle under her robes.

Heavy clouds were overcast and blackening the sky. A storm was brewing, and the wind was getting up.

'Looks like rain,' Danny said.

'Always rain in this country,' he moved on. Moving into the main square, it had started spitting. The clown woman was pushing her trolley through the town. She was a well-known figure, she wasn't homeless, but she was a bag lady. She collected things she found and put them in her trolly with the carrier bags full of rags. She dressed in burnt orange, her hair was matted and white, and she wore thick clown make up on her face. She always spooked you the first time you saw her. But the locals were used to seeing and smelling her, she wasn't dangerous. She was a fairly wealthy woman with her own home and was fairly well behaved, except she had an unfortunate habit of lifting her skirt and crapping in the middle of the street. But she spoke politely and logically despite this. So, the story goes she lost her children in a fire. She tried to save them but, in the attempt, she suffered serious burns and as a result, she took to hiding the burns behind a mask of clown makeup and wandered around the streets collecting rags.

Danny asked a man if he could help him out with a couple of quid. The man just shrugged his shoulders and pushed past him. Danny was going to have to improve his begging technique fast. Old habits die hard.

You could hear shouting swearing and barking dogs, Danny was on Rose Street next to Tesco and stood next to John.

'Sounds like something is kicking off,' John said.

There were ten of them. All of them were told they could live on a caravan site outside of town. They didn't come out much during the day. They looked like a gang of cutthroats, throwing back to the age of pirates as they swaggered through town intimidating shoppers and shoving people who got in their way. They had black eyes, scars on their heads and fists, and faces covered with teardrop tattoos. As they walked past the rough sleepers outside Mc Donald's they harassed them, picked up their sleeping bags and slung them in the street, and kicked their belongings around. One deliberately dragged a sleeping bag with his foot half-way down the high street and then kicked it to the curb.

'What ye looking at? Joey yer want my big cock up ye arse?' said one of them, who was swigging from a bottle of vodka.

Then without hesitating, he nonchalantly finished his bottle and casually slung it over his shoulder. It smashed into a million pieces on to the brick floor.

John went over to chat with Rupert who was waving his arms about demonstrating. Later in the day, John would be stealing from shops and mugging old ladies or selling himself in public lavatories. His desperation for a fix could turn him ugly, but that would all happen later in the day, once he'd got some drink down him.

Billy and Aaron were behind the group. Billy was on his pushbike, Aaron jogging beside him like a trainer and his boxing gorilla out on a run. Danny gave them a nod; they weren't his friends, but he didn't want to be their enemies. What was the saying, keep your friends close but your enemies even closer? Self-preservation. It seemed crazy that two months ago they had tried to kill each other and now it was water under the bridge. But that was just the way it was in his world. Danny thought they looked ridiculous, Billy pushing fifty and still riding around on their mountain bikes. Aarons once bright ginger hair now grey and twice as fat. They were both in and out of prison most of their adult lives. What wasted lives.

'We're looking for Yury, seen him at all?' asked Billy.

'No, saw him a few days ago up the park…why?'

'We'd just like a quiet word with him, that's all,' said Aaron.

'Private business. You see him, be sure to tell him,' said Billy.

'He'll want to know why.'

'OK, Dimitri is not a happy man, the park belongs to him.'

'Do they…I thought it belonged to the council.'

'He doesn't want anyone else selling their shit in the parks.'

'OK, I'll tell him, but he won't listen to me.'

'Just pass the message,' they jogged on.

Danny had heard about Dimitri, but he had never met him, and he didn't want to either. Dimitri was an Albanian criminal who was heavily into drugs, prostitution and people smuggling. He kind of controlled everything around here and he took his cut in one way or another. It was a secretive world that Danny wanted no part of.

Ten minutes later, all was quiet again. Rupert didn't want to press charges, the rough sleepers got their belongings back and the cleaners were busy trying to sweep up all the broken glass.

Sargent Tony Collins and Wallis were walking towards them, sweating in their stab vests.

'Morning gentlemen,' Tony said.

'Just cleaning up after the gypo bastards. Messy fuckers want shooting, best thing all round, line em up against the wall,' said Gerry the cleaner.

'Bit extreme,' said Wallis.

'Anyway, do you know about Paulina?' Tony asked Danny, who was watching Gerry sweep up on his day off because he had nothing better to do.

'Not heard anything,' he said.

'She's dead,' Tony replied.

'How?'

'Not sure. dragged her body out the river a few days ago. We think it was an accident.'

'Oh no, that's so sad. Poor Paulina. Such a waste.'

'But at least the disabled toilets will be cleaner, she used to take her fucking clients in there, spunk and shit all over the floor,' added Gerry

'Anyway, perhaps you could help us,' said Wallis, as she took a piece of paper out of her folder. It had a picture of an old lady on it that had gone missing. 'Have you seen this woman? she went missing from an old people home a couple of days ago. She's got Alzheimer's.'

Danny looked but he didn't recognise her.

'We're handing them out to anyone we think might be able to spot her, so if you see her call me immediately. You've got my number, but I'll write it out on here again just in case,' Wallis said.

'OK, got to dash. Call me sometime,' said Tony.

After the cleaners had swept up all the glass, Danny got himself a couple of pies from Greggs and sat down on the bench listening to today's musician. It was an older man who sang swing, a Frank Sinatra impersonator. He was singing white Christmas - in October. Danny saw Max walking towards him. He looked white as a sheet, all nervous and twitching.

'Alright boy?'

'Hello, you look terrified, are you alright?'

'It's all over fucking YouTube.'

'What is?'

'Me with me dick out waving me bare arse about in the park,' said Max.

'No way.'

'They filmed on their fucking phones and uploaded. It went viral and millions of people have seen it... that foreign bitch Magda spiked me tobacco. Gave me some wacky backy shit, thought it wasn't old Holborn that fucked me head up.'

'Have you seen her today?'

'No, and I don't wanna see her ever again. I'll slap her if I fucking do. Slag. I don't like her anymore. She can fuck off forever. That's it, I don't like the girl.'

'Really?'

'Nasty, rotten, lying, cheating, slapper, she can go to hell!'

'You don't mean that,' said Danny.

'You try to help someone and what happens. She chucks it back in yer face. She's beyond help. Three years in the nut house wouldn't sort her out.'

'She's beautiful,' Danny replied.

'Yeah, well I couldn't fuck a dog could I!'

'Did you?'

'No, I wanted to. I'm a man it's only natural. Not anymore.'

'Did you hear about Paulina?'

'What about her?'

'She died.'

'I saw her only last Monday.'

'Where?'

'None of your business.'

'I'd just like to know might be important,' said Danny.

'Fuck sake…in the toilets keeping her company, slapping her fat arse and watching it wiggle. See you later, maybe.'

'Bye,' replied Danny.

Then he saw the clown woman park her trolley outside a shop and walk into the main square. It was that the weekend shoppers would bear witness to a most unholy vision.

Horror was struck into the hearts of the people. The clown woman squatted in the middle of the road amidst shrieks and screams, hoisted up her dress and dumped a long thick pile of excrement from her arse on to the concrete and waddled off back to her trolly. There it sat on the ground, next to a pile of litter.

But some people didn't know what had caused all the commotion. Two girls walked past carefree, singing along to their iPod and smiling ear to ear, blissfully unaware of that freshly made crap they were walking towards. Danny was holding his sides, begging them to slip on it.

She held hands with her friend. Squelch! Right into it. She fell backwards into someone behind her. They both clattered to the ground crying and swearing, turning the air blue. Someone with a big pile of paper napkins came out from the coffee shop to assist her. She sat herself down on one of the chairs outside and tearfully wiped the mess off her foot.

Just another typical Sunday.

7

A group of rough sleepers were sitting on the bandstand drinking, smoking weed, yelling and screaming out; oblivious and ignorant. The bandstand was an old relic from the Victorian era, but no bands had ever played on it.

'Hello, my friend, you look like shit,' said Roman.

'Seen Magda?'

'Playground people fuck her like a dog for fifty pounds.'

'Magda?'

'Every person had this bitch goes like a locomotive,' said Roman, which sent sounds of crazed laughter reverberating round. Roman and Malik had not been in the city very long. A lot of homeless people live a transient lifestyle and one day they both turned up together. They began living rough up north, they then moved to the midlands and slowly worked their way south until they got here. They were both in their thirties, and both were heavy drinkers and drug users. They got into heavy bother with some dealers, so they came here to get away from them. Malik told Danny that one day the two of them jumped a dealer and stole all his gear and money, so they had to escape in case of reprisals. They were forever looking over their shoulders. Jimmy, on the other hand, had no such worries. He worked for Dimitri. Jimmy was just another member of Billy and Aarons crew, just another piece of scum who sold drugs in the city.

The girls from the church were approaching Marta and her company, suddenly the conversation stopped as they started to hand out food packages and cups of tea. Danny was offered a cup as usual but declined.

Malik turned on his radio loud as they listened to the crackle of some Bulgarian station. After the girls had left, they carried on talking.

'Dirty bitch whore,' said Malik.

'Lend me fifty pounds,' said Jimmy, as he shovelled a Cornish pasty into his mouth.

'Danny,' said Malik.

'What are you saying?' he replied.

'Would you like to fuck it?'

Danny remained quiet on the question.

'Maybe not,' said Roman, food fell out of his mouth like a pig. He was searching for a reaction, but he was going to be disappointed, Danny wasn't in the mood for it.

'Does she swallow it or spit it out?' Jimmy said, howling like a wolf as the others cracked up.

'Come, has she never fucked with you?' Malik asked as he was fiddling around with the radio controls, trying to get better reception.

'No,' Danny said, sending them into fits of hysterics.

'Not even suck?'

'No.'

The laughter died down. They were just having a joke with him and he didn't take it to heart until Jimmy said something.

'She had her legs wrapped around me neck the other night,

and I was so far up her the baby was giving me a blow job. That was below the belt.

A great rush of rage invaded Danny's brain. His body felt heavy and he could feel himself swaying under the pressure. He wanted to smash his fist into his face, right there and then.

Jimmy came right close up to him, invading his personal body space. 'Seriously, Danny, you didn't know she was a whore?'

'Well, at least I don't take it up the dirt box in public lavatories.'

'What did you say?'

'At least I don't sell my arse,' Danny replied bluntly.

Jimmy went for him, caught him straight in the jaw with an uppercut. Danny dropped like a ton of bricks on to the muddy earth. Malik and Roman grabbed Jimmy, trying to hold him back as he came to finish him off.

'He only jokes fuck sake,' Roman said as Danny got up.

'I am really sorry, Jimmy, I apologise. You can't help being a faggot.'

Jimmy broke free from their grip and lunged at Danny like a man possessed and smashed his fist into his head.

'Don't fuck with me,' he said, whilst being pulled off for the second time. It seemed to Danny that he was close to tears while he was sprawled out on the ground covered in mud. They all walked off and left him lying on the dirty slushy earth.

Danny turned his head to the side and looked up at the huge war memorial which dominated the park. It was all lit up. A huge bronze statue erected in the memory of the brave boys and men who gave their lives in the two wars. One of his uncle's names was on it. Private Robbie Welsh Died twenty-first of June, nineteen seventeen, aged twenty-three. There wasn't a single person over the age of thirty on that list of names.

Danny often wondered what he would be like if he were still alive. And what he would make of the city now. He couldn't drag his eyes away from them.

The restless polar wind began to gust and whipped across the park, waving the boughs of the trees whilst the huge black and twisted branches snapped above his head.

Jon's trolly had been left discarded next to the bandstand. It was crammed high with his junk; old broom heads, handles, a pair of crutches, umbrellas, and a dying radio could be heard playing somewhere underneath it all, the sound smothered by all his belongings and topped with his sleeping bag.

Danny went through the park and under the long echoing tunnel. You could hear the footsteps and voices fifty meters away a full minute before you saw the people. Graffiti was daubed all over the cream tiled walls and it was gloomy inside. The strip lighting which ran along the side of the tunnel kept flickering on and off. He could see Conner sitting on the floor. It looked like he was praying, but on closer inspection, he could see he was holding something in his hands.

'I think its shivering,' Conner said.

'What the hell is it?'

'Some sort of giant moth.'

'It's amazing.'

Danny had never seen the like of it in his life. They stood in the middle of the grimy subway, surrounded by dirt and filth, the walls defaced with obscene words and with this creature of beauty fluttering its wings in his open dirty palms. Soft delicate wings of deep green and purple.

'It must have been a big caterpillar,' said Danny.

'Maybe it's lost, maybe it flew over the sea from Africa.'

'Don't talk soft.'

It was strange, a bit like an omen or a sign. A beacon of light in a dark world.

'Where are you going to put it?'

'I'll keep it somewhere safe in case someone steps on it,' Conner replied.

Conner looked younger than his years, despite the huge mop of grey hair on his head. He really was an exception to the norm. He looked healthy and he had good teeth. Always a sign that living rough was all new to him. On the wall behind him, Danny read the latest message to Shaun from his family. It read, 'please come home Shaun we miss you we were here yesterday.'

Conner used to have a job and a flat. He was a good carpenter. He got his city and guilds certificate but when the bottom fell out of the building trade, he lost his job and couldn't pay his rent. His landlord wouldn't except benefit payments and gave him two months' notice to quit. He couldn't blame the landlord, he needed money himself. Then he couldn't find work. Too many students, too much foreign cheap labour - he said it was the same wherever you go. A lot of people felt that way.

Outside the subway, the cold air was screaming in Danny's face, blasting his skin with its icy blasts. Danny started to head up along the old city wall. Half-way along he stopped still and stared out across the city. The whole place was lit up by all the university buildings, office blocks, and right out across the horizon where the new theatre glowed. It changed from neon green, then purple and then red, like something from a batman movie. The view possessed a magical quality which lent it an air of mystery and betrayed its seedier side.

Sometime later, he found himself staggering around the backstreets of the city. He went around the back of Wilko stores, he thought she might be there. Sure enough, there she was, sitting on a bench in her torn dress. Her head was cut and there was dirt smeared across her drunk face. In a state of confusion, she looked up at Danny.

A lot of rough sleepers liked to kip down round the back of Wilko stores, there was a small labyrinth of alleyways and courtyards where the shops kept their wheelie bins, and so they would often chuck out a lot of decent grub boxed up or wrapped up. It was mainly uncontaminated tasty cakes, buns, and sandwiches, just past their sell by dates. It was safe and secluded with lots of little brick alcoves, just big enough for someone to bed down in like separate rooms in an open-air hotel. If you didn't sleep in a tent in the woods it was advisable to sleep in small groups near a security camera. Mainly for safety reasons. It could be dangerous if you were on your own. You could be an easy target for groups of drunken youths who may try to attack you or piss on you while you're asleep.

'You OK?' Danny asked.

'This shit situation. No like live on streets. Too much danger.'

'You like danger.'

'Not anymore. Maybe when I push this baby you try sex with my person, no prostitute. Maybe infection, but me no bitchy slag prostitute, no money. Everybody lies about me.'

Danny wasn't really listening because he felt emotionally drained.

'Where are you staying?'

'I was stay with Max, no like Max. He says please Magda sex all the time, but me no bitchy slag. He old man he try fuck me. Me no like this situation. Slap no try again.'

'What?'

'I disgusting.'

'Why?'

'I bad mother,' she whimpered. Danny held her hand and they just sat together. They didn't speak. Then she broke the silence.

'You smoke with me?' Magda unzipped her leather boot and rolled up a spliff. Danny said nothing. 'You smoke with me?'

'No.'

'Why not you my friend?'

'Of course, I am.'

'You hurt?'

'Jimmy.'

'I love you...too much.'

'You're hurt, you need go hospital,' Danny replied.

'No, no hospital. No police. Maybe pizza.'

'I don't believe you.'

'Please, tissue?'

Danny didn't have a tissue, so he let her blow her nose on his glove. When he got it back it was covered in thick green slime.

Just then, a girl walked past them with flashing boots. Magda screamed out, 'hey, baby, nice shoes!'

Magda got up pulled down her knickers and pissed all over the ground. Danny put his head in his hands.

'Don't worry, baby, just life. I take care of Max. Please ten pounds for Marijuana.'

Sometimes it was like her entire personality transformed.

Her looks, her demeanour, her entire being, altered in a flash of a second. She stood in front of him in her tight jeans, blue anorak, beret, and heavily made up face. She even walked differently. She strutted about smoking and swearing at him. Then she came right up to his face.

'Please just five pounds for drink?'

'I have none.'

'Please just five pounds, five pounds!'

'I gave you twenty a few days ago. I'll give you five.'

'I need twenty.'

'Haven't got twenty.'

'Please, you come drink with me.'

'No.'

'Need money for taxi.'

'No.'

'Yes.'

'Walk.'

'No, it too far.'

'Ten then.'

'Twenty?'

'No.'

'Need money for food. Go come cash.'

'Where?'

'Come cash! Come cash!'

'OK, I'll go to the cash point.'

It was dark and she stomped ahead of him. She didn't care. Danny went to the cash point and put in his card he had two hundred and fifty pounds in his account. Danny couldn't explain why but he took out one hundred. It left him one hundred and fifty pounds to last the next few weeks. At this rate, he would probably have to resort to bin raiding himself. He would probably have to get his tea from Marta. He gave her the one hundred.

'You have this?' she snatched it out of his hand.

'This is all I have. Do you understand?'

'Fuck sake!'

'No more.'

'Dickhead! Bye stupid,' she waddled off shaking her backside in the air, 'fucking dickhead,' she shouted.

In that moment, he hated her, but he hated himself for hating her.

8

Danny walked through the square and headed towards Mc Donald's. Magda was having a row with a group of girls. He had to stop her from getting her head kicked in, again.

Outside Mc Donald's, transvestites were parading around in their tightfitting blouses. They stomped up and down the pavement in their fish net tights and high heels, cackling, cat calling and propositioning old men for kicks. The late-night clubbers were there as well, trying to sober themselves up with hot coffee and cold air.

One girl, who was obviously the leader of the gang, shouted, 'you wanna slap?'

'Duh,' said Magda.

'Our fucking kill you. You slag! I'll rip your fucking head off!'

Magda smiled. She enjoyed the chaos. She was addicted to it.

'OK, look I'm sorry. I apologise for her, she can't help it,' Danny said.

'I'm not talking to you, I'm talking to your slag of a girl-friend. Apologise or we'll have to kick your head in.'

'Look, can't you see she is not right in the head. It's not her fault is it,' he said calmly, trying to defuse the situation.

There was a camera only six foot away and it would be

trained on them from the city watch control room.

'Not my problem. She should learn some respect.'

This girl didn't know the meaning of the word.

'Waaah! Harry give me too much FBI Hitler my grandad. Stop detective!'

'What did she say, did you understand that?'

'I told you, she's not well,' Danny replied.

'I having baby. King harry slap!' Magda screamed.

'Saint Judes,' said the girl.

'In and out all the time,' replied Danny.

'Sorry very much, you nice people. Me no bitchy slag, sorry,' Magda said. She then kissed the three girls, and all was forgiven.

'Go Salvation Army.'

'Salvation Army?'

'Yes, I like go church. Italian church, St Thomas.'

Spencer sat down in the small cramped office space, surrounded by shelves full of binders and reports. He was clutching hold of his two portfolios' like his life depended on it. He had outlined his proposal to Kenny, who sat stone faced throughout his pitch. He tried to look interested, but he had more pressing matters to think about.

Spencer showed off his glossy black and white prints of various depressed looking parks, full of depressed looking people sitting on park benches. People in varying states of inebriation; laughing, smiling, and pulling faces at the camera. There were old, grainy and atmospheric pictures of men bedded down in shop doorways as men in business suits and children walked past. Old men with wrinkled faces stroking their dogs.

He boasted of his art exhibitions which he had taken all over the country, his plan for an installation at the local library later this year, and all the money he had raised this year for charities such as 'Crisis at Christmas.' He told Kenny of the awareness he had made to the plight of the homeless and even showed him a photograph of himself standing outside Buckingham palace, presenting a check to the Prince of Wales.

He was working on a book, a photographic journal to be more precise, and was asking permission to take some photographs of the centre and some of the clients to publish within. He wanted to accompany the night outreach team to various locations to document the local wildlife, so to speak.

Kenny warned him of the dangers. He explained that a lot of people didn't like having their photos taken, someone poking a camera in their face asking questions. Many of the homeless didn't want anyone knowing they were even on the streets and the last thing they wanted on earth is to be in his book.

Spencer assured Kenny that he would ask peoples permission before taking any pictures and would treat the whole exercise with the upmost anonymity and respect.

'I assure you, Kenny, I only have their best interests at heart and I would do nothing to jeopardise that.'

'I will ask on your behalf, understood?'

'Understood.'

'Don't go waking around at night by yourself and don't approach any large groups drinking in the parks, it's not advisable.'

'I promise, I want to work with you, not against you.'

Was he really interested in the plight of the homeless, or was he only really interested in boosting his ego and showing of his glossy images at his exclusive champagne gatherings in

Knightsbridge, with only a fraction of the money going to the charity?

The clients were piling through the doors like a long line of Sherpa's, carrying everything they owned on their backs.

A group of men and women were shuffling about outside the church door, armed with torches and throwing moving shadows across the porch floor. Father Dylan stood leaning far too close to sister Josephine. They passed them both and went inside.

Just inside the door was a table spread with fruit bread and a jug of orange squash.

'Beautiful church,' Magda said, and walked in a vacant haze. She then poked about in a box next to the table, took out a paper cross and gave it to Danny. 'For you,' she said.

In the adjacent room, all the tables and chairs had been rearranged to form one long seating area in an attempt to bring people together. At the far end of the table, Danny saw Terry with Jodi on his lap, holding up a sprig of mistletoe. They were sucking one another's face off.

The lights were flicked, and the shelter shone bright from a stream of Christmas lights that ran from all four corners of the building and along the sides of the walls. The chairs stretched along the sides of the tables started to fill up.

Plates piled up high with sausage, bacon, eggs, mushroom, beans, and fried bread. The gorgeous smell of fried bacon filled the room and the steam from the plates curled high up to the ceiling, then dissipated.

Plates started to be passed around and people began stuffing their faces and draining the coffee while Christmas music played. Everyone talked excitedly and cracked obscene jokes with one another. Some more people arrived out of the cold with flushed cheeks and watery eyes. A long queue formed and the volunteers in the kitchen were shouting out orders. 'More eggs, more beans, more mushrooms, more everything!'

Some orders were lost in translation, so people started to do mimes. Romanians were clucking like chickens for eggs, grunting like pigs for bacon, but nobody knew how to make a sound like a mushroom.

There had to be near on sixty people inside. Rucksacks, blankets, and sleeping bags were strewn everywhere along the walls and piled up on top of each other. When everyone had finished their plates, they were all gathered up and piled on the counter to be washed up.

The air was thick with foreign accents, all merging together to create one massive wall of sound.

Joe was sat next to the door. A known troublemaker, serial shop lifter, and drug addict. He was all over city watch radio, and every time he came onto the shopping centre security had to drag him away. In fact, most of the people in this room caused trouble at the shopping centre.

Next to him sat john. John was recently released from prison and is currently on bail for alleged assault and battery. He has been diagnosed with borderline personality disorder and needs help to break free from a cycle of prison, street, drugs, shoplifting, then prison.

Kelly sat opposite. A beautiful girl once, about thirty. A drug addict and prostitute. She was sent to prison a month ago for shoplifting and she had just been released. She's been on the streets for five years. A long history of heroin abuse, having first used when she was just fourteen. She's currently on meth. She wants to get clean. She's been doing it too fucking long. Her words. She's lost count of how many times she's been inside, but its most of her adult life. She's scared to stop using and unable to without secure accommodation, yet she claims she's better able to cope inside than out. She wants rehab but has been told she can't due to not engaging with support services in the past. She has been diagnosed with schizophrenia, bipolar, substance abuse, psychosis, and even labelled a psychopath. Besides her other drugs, she is on a daily medication of diazepam, paroxetine, quetiapine and denzapine. She literally rattles when she walks.

Martin sat next to her. He has been a heroin and crack user, on and off, for almost twenty years. He was clean once for five years but has been in and out of prison since the age of sixteen. He's been using since he was twenty. He says it keeps him warm at night and is his preferred choice of pain killer.

Martin got out of prison six months ago after serving his sentence for ABH and he was looking for a return ticket. It won't take him long to find one. He liked prison as his friends were there. He had three square meals a day and a roof over his head, which was more than he had here.

Recently, a man stabbed a complete stranger to death in a subway because he just wanted to go back inside. He had a reputation in jail. He was respected, feared even. On the outside he felt insignificant and unable to cope.

Thomas sat on the floor. He was given a fifty-day prison sentence for breach of probation. He served forty. On the day of his release he overdosed on spice. He suffers from anxiety, depression, epilepsy and has hepatitis. He has always committed drug related crime but says if he could keep clean, he would stop fucking about. He is on anti-psychotics and mood stabilisers. He also has a split personality disorder. He self-harms all the time and has cuts all over his wrists and arms. He says it gives him release and proof of existence. He is another one lost in a vicious cycle.

Danny looked up and around the walls of the centre, which were decorated with banners and Christmas lights. There was a tree in the corner with a pile of unwrapped presents underneath and donations from the well-meaning public.

Some people were down at the far end of the building practising silly Christmas carols. The God squad Christian volunteers kept popping out to pray for people. Danny didn't care for them much.

John was playing table tennis with Harry and Keith was lounging on the easy chair stroking his white boxer. Keith reminded Danny of a character out of a Charles Dickens novel. I think it was his small diminutive stature and his quintessential white boxer. Most street people had dogs for companionship, but mostly for protection. Some people might think it was cruel, but the dogs were mostly well fed and looked after.

The ping pong ball flew off the table and bounced down the room. John went to chase after it. There were about thirty rough sleepers in this evening. Most had addiction problems and mental health issues. A few worked. The centre had a strict no drink and no drugs policy, so you never saw the really wild ones. Over half were from eastern Europe.

It was a good place. They gave you breakfast, lunch, an evening meal in the winter, and a bed for the night. They had showers, laundry facilities and counselling services who helped with housing and art therapy. You could even go online and find a job if you wanted. The staff were firm, but fair.

The ping pong ball settled between the feet of Fred who was still twenty years later, busy ranting about the aliens to anyone unfortunate enough to find themselves sitting next to him.

'The Queen and the Duke of Edinburg are shape shifters who drink human blood to look like us. Half human and half alien creatures have infiltrated us. They are both giant lizards!' Fred yelled.

John had to crawl under the table to retrieve the ball, where he noticed Fred wearing the new boots he has found him.

'Thanks for the boots!' He shouted across the room.

Barry was finding it very difficult to play a game of trivial pursuit with Thomas, as he thought he knew the answer to every question despite what it said on the card. He would argue the point until you gave in. Keith was shouting at Fred to leave his washing alone as he was unzipping his laundry bag and having a good poke around. Then he started to pull out some of the items of clothing and waving his smalls about for everyone to see, making sniffing sounds and pulling faces. Then he pulled out a pair of Keith's pants and put them on his head. Keith went over to Fred, grabbed his underpants of his head, and started stuffing his washing back into his bag. Fred pulled out a pair of women's frilly knickers and red brazier and began waving them about in front of everyone. Everyone was gawking. Keith claimed he was only doing the washing on a woman's behalf, due to her being barred.

Sam and Jodi were back in the centre, they had been housed three months ago but were back living on the streets again.

Some people who did live on the streets went to visit their families at Christmas, and a lot of their families didn't even know they were living on the streets. Pride can make you do strange things. People would lie to their parents or children. They would pretend they were working overseas and had a good job rather than admit they had lost everything and were living in a tent in the woods. Some people had been lying to their families for years and some people find it hard to adjust to a normal life. It happens a lot. They can't cope with living in a flat, they miss their friends, can't find work and forget to pay the bills or burn the place down.

Sister Josephine sat down next to Harry but that old lecherous priest, Father Kelly, had his eyes fixed on her like glue, looking her up and down. She noticed and felt troubled by him. She held Harry's hand under the table and Harry felt an unnatural urge churn in his lower regions. The priest gazed into her eyes. She didn't look at him. More and more he leered at her, appealing to her. The pressure inside him was building and she could tell. She turned a whiter shade of pale, which is no mean feat for a Nigerian.

Garry was putting up a new poster. John was going into hospital and needed someone to look after his dog. The notice board was rammed, so he had to rearrange all the other notices in a fashion so it could fit in. Jam packed with missing posters, therapy groups, hostel information leaflets, and job opportunities. He had to lap them all over each other until there weren't any corners showing. He nearly ran out of space and drawing pins.

Frank came in from the toilets and announced they were flooded. Gary went into the cleaning cupboard and came out with a mop and bucket, and then went into the gents.

Three minutes later, he emerged from the toilets holding a mop in one hand and a bottle of scotch in the other, carrying an expression of someone who had just had a red-hot poker stuck up their arse.

'Found this in the cistern,' he said. Everyone looked around sheepishly. All you could hear were the pipes cough and splutter.

Danny went into the main church, looked up and around at the carved walls and up into its rafters which were covered with cobwebs. There was even a bird which flitted from place to place. It was in desperate need of restoration. It was empty as they were all outside singing stupid songs.

There was a long central corridor which separated the rows of pews leading up to a marble statue of Christ, and a church organ with a piano next to it.

Magda was sat down at the piano. She lifted the lid and started to play. Trying to remember the notes, slowly she got control of the rhythm. Danny didn't recognise the tune, but it was classical. It was beautiful; such sensitivity. Someone must have taught her to play like that. He had a lump in his throat, and he could feel himself welling up. He began to sob; he couldn't control himself. She played louder. Such a melancholic melody, floating away. She stopped.

'Why you cry… stop cry. No cry in church. You man, not baby. I don't remember the name this song, I play for pope in Vatican. I forget what it's called, maybe Mozart, Schubert? No, Chopin.' She got off the piano stool and sat next to him on the pew. For the first time ever, she kissed him gently on the lips, she then took his hands and pressed them against her chest.

'Wait,' Danny said.

'Shh, zip it.'

'But-'

'Zip.' She moved her hands down his front and kissed him on the mouth, moving her tongue around inside his lips. She kissed his eye lids, his ears, his neck, and then she moved her hand between his legs and squeezed him. He groaned.

'Shh, quiet. Not loud,' Danny was having the strangest thoughts in his head. His heart was hammering, he felt a swelling in his pants, and she had a look of passion on her face. 'Why you scare? Don't worry,' she squeezed him again.

'We are in church.'

'Doesn't matter,' she said.

Danny kissed her back. Mouth, eyes, neck, and ears. Then she stood up abruptly and walked into the toilet. Danny followed her and stood in the doorway as she hoisted up her dress and went for a pee.

'Look what you've done to me,' he said, and turned sideways to show her his erection under his trousers.

'Dickhead!' Magda snarled venomously, then got up flushed the chain. 'Dickhead!' Then she looked at him dreamily and pushed him up against the wall. She unbuckled his belt, pulled his trousers down and squeezed him again, then started tugging hard on him. He had to ask her to stop.

'Stop please, too hard.'

She stopped looked at him with disgust. 'Dickhead, stupid dickhead.'

He did himself up, then Magda pushed against him again. She squeezed him, pinned him hard against the wall and kissed him. Then she gave him a long, hard, psychopathic glare and put her hand around his throat and started to throttle him.

'Wanky dickhead! Wanky dickhead!' Magda screamed. She started laughing hysterically laughing, and then she let go. She stroked Danny's hair tenderly, kissed his forehead and said, 'sorry baby.'

Time to go.

9

'Pavel!' Danny shouted.

On his way home he spotted him lying face down underneath the clock tower. He awoke. The righthand side of his faced had swollen up and there was blood in his mouth. Scrabbling about on all fours, he lifted himself up. Two drunk women like alley cats walked past him and began to screech out relentlessly into the night.

'Bastard, look at these bastards! I hate these bastards… you like my underwear?' Pavel pulled down his trousers and waved his backside at them. 'Look at me! They should be shot for looking like whore.'

Over on the bench, Rupert sat rocking back and forth whilst clutching his heart and wheezing.

Dong! Dong! Dong! Chimed the clock tower bell.

Pavel stood next to the clock tower and began jabbing at the air with his fists. He made punching sounds as he shimmed, ducked and weaved, waving his head about and punching at the air in front of him, throwing left and right hooks and upper cuts.

Rupert got off his bench and walked across to where they were standing.

'My father was a boxer,' he said. 'But he never raised his fists to me, not once. My mother or father never spoke to me much either. They never spoke to each other the whole time I lived with them. Twenty years of silence. We had the tv, sometimes we watched that. On or off made no difference, the silence sent me crazy.'

He went back to his bench and started crying and wailing into the night. Pavel stopped punching the air.

Pavel told Danny that he was a Latvian army boxing champion. He didn't believe it. He didn't believe most of the stories people told him about themselves. A lot of street people lived in cloud cuckoo land and made up stories about themselves. He couldn't blame them.

Pavel always wore army surplus clothes and told people he was ex special forces. He would say, 'I'm not allowed to talk about it,' and then he would relate some story or another about how he saved his entire army unit running down five enemy machine gun posts, single handed.

'Look, crazy woman!' Danny turned around and saw Magda. She was staggering and had a bump on her head.

'Fucking hell! What happened,' he asked.

'People punch me. Not my fault why people punch me. I good person.'

'Did you punch them first?'

'Maybe.'

'You have to be careful.'

'Huh, be careful. This all you say.'

'You're an intelligent person, a good person. Change or you'll go to court again you'll get deported.'

'No deportation. Council give me home. Maybe London.

Stupid council…why not here.'

'London is not far. It's a home.'

'I want live here.'

'You turn down everywhere, you can't keep turning down places. They're trying to help you. You have to take what they offer. Do you want to live on the streets forever? Do you want to be an old woman living on the streets, because that will happen?'

'Maybe I stay with you in hostel?'

'You can stay, for a small time. But you can't tell anyone.'

'You my friend, forever. Not Harry, not max, just you.'

'You have to stop drink and drugs.'

'Easy.'

'You want to stay tonight?'

'No, not now. This is not possible.'

'Where you go now?'

'I go speak Angus.'

'Who's Angus?'

'This person, like witch doctor herbalist. They give me medicine for pain for relax woman pregnant, much pain here and here,' she touched Danny on the lower back and between the shoulder blades. 'Angus says I can sleep with his person. No sex, just friend.' She went. Danny just hoped he wouldn't give her too much medicine.

Tramping through the streets, you usually can't move for rough sleepers and buskers or as some people liked to call them, beggars with guitars. The same for the survey makers, the religious collectors, big issue sellers, and chuggers. If you were to give your money to all of them, it wouldn't last very long. Some of the buskers were good, some were downright awful, playing everything from Mozart on violins to Motorhead on traffic cones. Then Danny heard the familiar sound of an acoustic guitar being played. He half recognised the tune. As he got closer, he saw Johnny with his guitar case on the ground full of coppers and penny chews. He dropped some money in it.

Johnny came from Blackburn, originally. He could sing and he could play, unlike Rory. Danny would just sit down and listen on occasions, then he would throw him a pound. It was quite amusing because Johnny grew up in the same street as one of the locals, PC Wallis, and they had both moved down here. She nicked him for busking up north, and down south. It was a pure coincident. But Johnny always tells people that she's stalking him. Johnny always dressed in black leather, except in the summertime when the sun comes out and he gets the over-whelming desire to strip right down to only his boxer shorts and sandals.

'Cheers matey,' said Johnny. Danny stood next to him and listened a while until he stopped. 'What I really need is a proper band, you know, the whole ensemble. It sounds much better with a drum and whistle, you can't really do it justice with just a guitar,' he continued.

'Can't you find anyone to play with?'

'Not with that money, hardly got enough for a bag of chips,' replied Johnny.

Danny could see Brendan slowly shuffling down the street towards them with a beer tray in his hand which he probably just half inched from Weatherspoon's.

'You forgot the beers,' Johnny said.

'I'm cheap. What songs can you play?' Brendan replied.

'I prefer to play my own songs, well, poetry really.'

'See one of these,' he showed him the tray, 'you can get a really cracking sound out of one of these things. They've been using these things for generations; I'll count you in. And a one, two, three, four-'

Johnny sang and Brendan banged the tray, keeping time as he played and slamming the beer tray against his head. Danny wouldn't say Johnny had the most dulcet tones; it was more like a nasally whine. Musically, he had an unusual delivery and at times he sounded like a Dalek. The words left a lot to desire.

Brendan banged the tray over Danny's head until he had a migraine, but it was working. Soon they had a whole crowd of people surrounding them and throwing money. He thrashed out another tune on his head and on the heads of passing drunks, some of whom danced a jig for the growing audience.

The chorus was hopeless, but they were a big hit. By now, Brendan's head was swelling and bruised, but it was worth it. He asked them to stop the banging and started to gently strum, and the crowd listened intently as he began to sing less harshly with a more pleasing voice.

'Jimmy didn't have a toilet in his flat... So, he had to crap on his living room mat... The shit and the piss grew higher and higher... And now it looks like a giant quagmire... The neighbours complained of the dreadful smell... As it seeped under the door and down the stair well... They said to the council this is absurd... We keep slipping on poor Jimmy's turd... So, the council moved Jim to a posh bed sit... Were he could have a less disruptive shit... But Jimmy missed all the fun of catching his neighbours on the run... So, he wiped his bum on copies of The Sun.... And posted them through their letter boxes, one after one.'

They split the money three ways, he said it was the best pay day in months. The crowd loved the tunes and had a good laugh.

'Seen that crazy bird of yours lately,' Johnny asked.

'She's spending the night with Angus,' replied Danny.

A look of dread came over Johnny's face. 'Look matey I've heard bad things about that Angus, really bad things.'

'Like what?'

'He's got more drugs than Pfizer. I have heard from several people that he likes to drug up girls and have his evil way with em, but they never remember owt afterwards.'

'What?'

'Sometimes he gets his mates round too. He's evil but there is never any proof.'

'Shit, no way.'

'Yes way. You want me to go there with you?'

'I dunno where he lives.'

'Neither do I.'

They set out to try and find him. The town felt more intimidating at night. The streets were filling up with drunk students and the usual idiots who were out looking for trouble. They wouldn't have a good night until they found it. They were walking around like they meant business, while a panda car slowly cruised up the high street keeping a look out.

Thumping music was blasting through the night sky. There was a group of people outside the library talking, smoking, drinking cans of beer, and generally fooling around to the heavy thumping beat of a CD player. Danny saw Pavel in a pair of trousers, shirtless and shivering. Danny felt too warm, he had three jumpers on, so he took one of his off and gave it to him. 'You can borrow this, but I want it back.'

Pavel took it. The others were wrapped up in their smoking drinking and dancing to take too much notice.

'Do you know where Angus lives?' Danny asked.

'Hippy Angus?'

'Yes,' said Johnny.

'He used to be a friend of mine till he sleep with my cousin and give her drugs.'

'Where does he live?'

'Angus?'

'Yes.'

He just shrugged.

They went back through the city streets and passed Frank sitting in Mc Donald's doorway, shouting at himself as he gulped down vodka. He was a big man and he looked like a monster, but he wasn't one. The left-hand side of his face had dropped due to a bad operation, so his eyes didn't level up. Well, there was just a hole for his right eye, all closed up. He had a big dent on his forehead in the shape of a household iron and a circular scar on his cheek. He sat outside the entrance of the takeaway in a bright orange high viz jacket, with his ruck sack spilt all over the ground and a bottle of cider beside him. His name was Terry, but everyone called him Frank - short for Frankenstein. He was sitting next to Beth. She was not a dwarf, but not far off it. They were a couple. She was the complete opposite to Frank, who was well over six foot even with his hunched shoulders. Her head barely reached above his waist. Beth liked to set fire to peoples tents after she had stolen items from inside them.

They didn't know where angus lived.

A couple were having a very loud domestic outside Mc

Donald's, shouting at each other in a foreign language.

It was always busy outside Mc Donald's, morning, noon and night. You would think there was nowhere else to eat. The regulars were outside chatting and stuffing their faces and kids who looked about ten were smoking fags with their mates. The ground was washed with litter.

The woman got up abruptly from her seat and tipped the table over coca cola flew everywhere

'Kurwa spierdolic!' She screamed. She picked up her chair and it flew through the air, crashing into the bin.

The whole crowd slowly pushed back to create a space. A big security guard pushed himself through the crowd.

'Stop now!' He yelled. Then he made a grab for the woman and pushed her against the wall. She shrieked. Her fella was up like a shot, trying to pull him off her while another security guard tried to pull her fella off of him. The guard got his arm behind the man's back and forced him to the ground. A third guard came running. The woman jumped on his back. He twisted her around and around until she fell off, he then grabbed her and started dragging her across the floor, yelling and cursing. His colleague was sitting on her fella, slowly squeezing the air out of his lungs. The other two now struggling with the woman, trying to grab her arms and legs. He eventually managed to restrain her while she was screaming abuse at everyone.

Danny didn't have time to hang around and watch. There was a woman standing on the street corner stopping people as they passed and asking them questions. She was holding a piece of paper in her hand, it looked like a map or perhaps a picture of some kind. As Danny got closer, she stopped him and showed him a picture of a man.

'Excuse me, have you seen this person?' She asked him, then showed him the picture. The person on the photograph was unmistakeable and his name was written in large letters underneath; 'ROBBIE.'

'Have you tried the parks or the police station? He calls himself Jonah now, what's he done?' Danny looked at her, scrutinising her face. 'I hope you don't mind me asking, but who are you?'

'I'm his daughter,' she replied.

It was a shock to hear that. You sometimes forget that most of the rough sleepers have, or have had, families before in their previous lives. But he didn't have time to chat.

'Sorry, I have to go. Maybe try the-'

She cut him short. 'My mother is sick. I don't think she's got long to go. Please, I have to find him,' she pleaded.

This put Danny in somewhat of a dilemma, but he had to help, and he knew where he was likely to be.

It didn't take long to find him. The best way to describe his doorway was like a cross between a shrine and Santa's grotto. He was another collector of junk who pushed around all his belongings in an old shopping trolly. He wore brightly coloured, long and flowing robes with bells and ribbons sewn on. He had long hair, a beard and looked like a wizard. Robbie used to have a flat, but he accidently burnt it down. Most of the time he was confused, zoned out of his mind on weed and playing the kazoo or ranting like a maniac. He was ranting like a maniac when they found him.

He stopped dead when he saw them. They left them to reacquaint themselves.

'Hey, buddy,' it was Martin sitting in a shop doorway, wrapped up in a green sleeping bag. 'How you doing?'

'Fine,' Danny replied.

'Oh, so fucked up, insecure, neurotic, and emotional.'

'That's about it,' Danny replied. He sat down next to him and buried his head in his hands. Danny was cold now, he wished he hadn't given his spare jumper to Pavel, but he wasn't going back for it.

Martin reached into his battered canvas bag and took out a heavy looking jumper, then tossed it over to Danny. 'Keep it,' he said.

'Sorry, Danny, I've got to get back to hostel for curfew,' said Johnny, 'good luck.'

Martin was as pale as a ghost. He was gaunt looking with sunken cheeks and a large nose which made him look like a starving sparrow. He hadn't cut his hair in months; he had let himself go and that was an understatement, but his dog was in excellent health.

People petted the dog and pitied him. Martin's legs were so thin that he hardly had the strength to stand up, and his hands were red and bloated, covered in calluses. It looked like he would probably be next to pop his clogs. He used to be a mod, judging by his green bomber jacket, which was covered in old badges from various rally's, but they were old now and fading away to nothing. Just like himself.

Gradually they heard the overhead noise of a helicopter which built to a deafening crescendo. It felt like it was practically on top of them. The air vibrated between the rota blades like the amplified sound of wasps. Like a colossal beating wave, it continued for about a minute, projecting a beaming light across the night sky.

'Police,' Danny said.

'They're probably looking for Magda.'

'So am I, she's with some bloke called Angus. She might be in danger.'

'Hippy Angus, Mr Rufus Date rape?'

'Yes, you know where he lives?'

'Oh yeah!'

After walking half a mile, Danny turned left, passed Domino's pizza and through a narrow alley way into a large housing estate. The light from the modern houses shone ribbons of golden light.

He saw a group of lads approaching him. There was probably no need to worry, just relax, he told himself, it might be local students who weren't looking for trouble. There were a few little street gangs in the city that liked to cause trouble. One in particular. They were kids really, that liked to swan around and look intimidating. They dressed in black and hung around in large groups around the parks and the edges of estates. They would cycle up and down on their mountain bikes, pick fights with foreigners, steal from shops and commit petty crime in attempt to gain individual notoriety among their peers. Occasionally, people would get hurt. They thought they were tough, but they were just stupid little kids in Danny's opinion. Stupid little kids who needed to grow up.

Danny saw a girl. He didn't know if she was drunk or drugged. A young lad was trying to carry her along the path, followed by four stony faced youths on their bikes, all dressed in black with scarfs around their faces. She was vulnerable, without a doubt.

'You need any help mate?' Danny asked.

'No, it's OK mate. She's OK, don't need no help,' one replied as they passed him.

At least he asked, Danny thought to himself.

'Get her to the hospital, I don't think the taxi drivers will take her,' he heard another say.

They headed down the slope in the direction of the park. The young lad was struggling a bit with her, but he seemed genuinely concerned for her well-being, whatever the matter was. Danny watched them take her down to towards the park. She stood up, but she was very wobbly. Then she fell over and they crowded around her.

I can't interfere. I can't save the world. Maybe I should let it go. I get into enough trouble sticking my nose into other people's business. Danny thought.

He stayed put for a few minutes and waited quietly, watching the group by the benches. He couldn't see what was going on with the girl because she was obscured from view by the group of lads on bikes. Then he could see the security approaching in their high viz jackets, gleaming in the dark. So, he continued.

'I'm seeing, Magda, I think I've shot my load. Was here four weeks ago, had some Russian bitch. Angus gets me loads of birds, never had Magda before. My little fellas begging for it,' a strange man told him as he stood outside the flat.

Danny ignored him and shouted up at the window. No answer. So, he pushed open the door.

'Hey, I'm before you! Wait!' Said the stranger.

Danny ran up the stairs to flat five and kicked open the door. The he saw them. Magda and Angus wrapped up in each other. Her body looked lifeless; he had her slumped like a rag doll bent over his bed. She was groaning. Danny looked into her half-shut eyes as he moved inside her. His heart burst. Adrenalin drooled into his brain and rage consumed him.

Danny lifted him off her and threw him off the bed. He banged his head hard on the edge of a bedside table. Dazed, drugged, and confused, he scrambled about naked on all fours.

'Scum!' Danny yelled, as he checked Magda. He stroked her hair and shook her gently. She moaned and her eyes flickered.

'You arsehole! You bastard!' Danny screamed.

'Relax, have some weed,' Angus replied.

'Fucking rapist bastard!'

'No.'

'Yeah!'

Angus crawled over to his armchair and slumped down. He didn't seem the least bit concerned. Danny was leaning over Magda trying to wake her up, but she was out of it.

'What did you give her?'

'I don't er remember.'

'I want to know, now.'

'I can't tell you.'

'Won't or can't? Come on, just tell me!'

'I don't know!'

Danny looked around the room. It was a mess. There were packets of weed wraps and all kinds of bottles with pills inside them. He saw a battered rucksack on the floor. More pills. He slung it across the room, its contents flying out across the floor.

'You're a sick man,' Danny said.

'It's only natural.'

'She's about to drop!'

'Makes it better.'

'You are scum!' Danny saw an empty bottle of whiskey on the floor, grabbed it and smashed it against the wall. It shattered. Glass flew everywhere. He held it against Angus' throat and let out a shriek of fear.

'Wa-wa-wait,' he stuttered, 'let go, please don't hurt me.' He was panic stricken and gulped for air. 'You're fucking mad!'

'Probably, but you're despicable.'

'You don't have to do this.'

'What you give her?'

'She wanted it... she consented. She was a willing partner.'

Danny dropped the bottle, picked him up off the chair and pulled him over to her.

'Look at her...look what you've done. She just wanted some medicine for her back and somewhere to sleep. She trusted you, but you had other ideas. You knew she wouldn't do it willing, so you had to drug her first. Do you know how they treat rapists in prison? You could go inside for ten years.'

'On what evidence? She won't go to the cops.'

'No, but I will.' Danny threw his naked body against the wall. He picked himself up, sat against the wall and started quivering. Magda was dead to the world, moaning on the bed. Danny covered her over with a duvet, then the service bell rang. He picked it up. It was the nerd from out in the street, he wanted to know if Angus had finished with Magda. 'Angus says fuck off,' Danny put down the intercom.

'Please don't call the police,' Angus cried. He looked nervous and pathetic sitting naked against the wall, whimpering.

Danny picked him up off the floor and pinned him against the wall by his throat. He started to laugh. His cut was getting worse and it was dripping all over his feet.

'What are you laughing at?' Danny said.

He stopped laughing and started to scream, so Danny gave him a slight whack around the head to shut him up. He dropped to the floor and huddled up into a ball. Danny picked him up, opened the door and pushed him naked into the hallway. Then he went over to the bed and cradled Magda in his arms. He gently put her down again, all the time he could hear Angus crying and banging on the door. Danny got out his mobile and dialled a number and waited for a reply.

'Hello, Tony Collins speaking.'

'Tony, its Danny. I need your help. I dunno what to do I'm with Magda. I can't wake her up, think she's taken something. I dunno what, she's unconscious in some flat. Someone's raped her, there's drugs all over the shop. It's an emergency!'

'OK just slow down. Breathe. Where are you?'

'Seven Chepstow house.'

'OK. I'm on my way.'

Danny heard sirens wailing and saw light flashing from emergency vehicles, as they drew outside the beam swept passed the window and fell across him in a blue flicker. She seemed to have stopped breathing.

Danny tried his best to revive her, but he couldn't. All feeling flooded from within him. Shock set in. He took slow, deep breaths, and composed himself, as he knelt over her lying on the bed. The whole room flashed blue. Danny looked out the window and saw Angus, still naked, being bundled into the back of a police car. He then heard muffled yells as the police made their way up the staircase, then muttering outside the door before they burst through.

The paramedics came first. They started working on her, checking for a pulse and airways for vital signs of life. 'Do you know what she's taken?'

'No,' Danny said, trembling and covering his face with his hands.

'Magda, what have you taken mate. Magda, Magda, can you hear me love?'

No response.

They started breathing into her mouth and thumping her chest. They kept breathing. They kept thumping. Then they charged up the portable defibrillators.

'Stand aside.'

The jolts of electricity charged through her lifeless body. Danny felt the pain. He felt it charge out. With a stale heart in his mouth, he tried to dislodge the image with his mind, but he couldn't. He felt like he was staring death in the face. They carried on.

She coughed. Her eyes flickered and she lay on the bed looking at Danny in a trance, her eyes big as saucers and hair all over the place. She groaned. Nausea crept against Danny's lungs as he stood in the blue flickering light, speechless.

'Danny, I know it's going to be hard, but you have to walk away from this,' Wallis said.

'She's like a Bugatti Veyron with bicycle breaks,' said Tony.

'OK. We need to get her up. One, two, three, lift,' they said as they lifted her on to the stretcher.

Quiet again, Danny watched the paramedics take Magda downstairs and load her into the back of the ambulance and drive away.

10

The roads were frozen over and the street cleaners had been putting down grit all morning. By the afternoon, only small trickles of water ran down the sides from the melting piles of ice and sludge.

The procession marched like an advancing army towards the cathedral, battling against a north easterly wind that blew endlessly. It was heavy going and it was getting heavier by the second. Danny followed the crowd of poor deluded people, in his opinion, who were moving at a slug's pace.

They were singing and full of joy. All of their minds had been twisted and fed into believing their souls would be saved and blessed. The sick and the lame be healed. The vision of Mary, which appeared five hundred years ago, was no more real or sacred than the plastic effigies and glow in the dark crucifixes that hung around their necks. But they believed, happy or deluded, who was he to criticize. I suppose, when there is so much pain and suffering in the world, you need something to believe in. No doubt the cathedral would bear witness to overcoming joy and the kissing of the blessed virgin's feet, and the crying and the fainting. Thought Danny.

There were young and old, rich and poor, black and white people. Some on crutches, many in wheelchairs and some people were doing the pilgrimage barefoot. They walked with cuts and blisters, first aid kits at the ready and laughing all the way while someone else watching in a nice warm office laughed all the way to the bank.

'Promises of miracles this way please make a large donation,' a sign said. Hymns, psalms, prayers and nonstop singing with such passion and joy. The wind howling over them and screaming in their faces. Gerry and Danny trying to push themselves through everything.

Danny stopped for a rest by a pillar and watched the advancing masses wrapped with exhaustion as they passed by.

'Aghhh, shut the fuck up!' Gerry screamed his lungs out, cutting short their musical renditions, as he waved his arms in the air frantically. 'Shut the fuck up!'

At first, they were silenced by the shock of his outburst, as a man shifted about and fumed in his wheelchair, but soon had they ceased their singing they had started up again.

'What is this, why my life just problems. Wanky council,' Magda just jumped out in front of Danny and screamed like the wind in his face. 'No accommodation, merry Christmas.'

'But you are having a baby in a week?'

'I know!'

'I don't understand why they do not help you. You're pregnant, you live in tent.'

'I know, please gun end this now, dickhead council! They promise me what? I have baby in tent, maybe I die.'

'What can you do?'

'I don't know, I have to stay with your person short time. You speak with probation, maybe better. No time, no nappy, no powder, no cosmetic for Joseph. Where you sleep, on floor?

'Fuck sake, no more children, no more pregnant. Why I not have abortion, why I not kill this child. This man, Angus, give me ecstasy now this problem. Danny please give me money, marijuana, I stress,' she started crying.

Danny held her as more people shuffled past them. 'I'll see you after work, by clock tower,' he said, then gave her twenty pounds. She gave him a packet of sweets and off she went.

Just then, Tony Collins came around the corner. 'Danny are you OK mate? You don't look good.'

'It's, Magda, I dunno what to do. She's gonna have the baby any minute and she hasn't got anywhere to live. I need your help, it's an emergency. Can't you do something?' Danny felt himself welling up.

'She's not done herself any favours,' said Tony. 'They have offered her places, but she's turned them down. They tried to help, and they can't do anymore. She wants to live here but there's no place for her here, there are more deserving people.'

'More deserving?'

'They won't give her a place here. She can't look after herself, how's she gonna look after a baby. The baby will be taken into care, she must know this. If it was that bad, she would take anywhere, its four walls, it shouldn't matter where it is.'

'Yes, but she's not right in the head. Can't you section her or something, or find her a bed at the mental hospital?

'Why, has she threatened to kill herself?'

'Not exactly.'

'The courts decided that she is capable of making her own decisions, it's not that simple. She tries to manipulate the police, the courts, probation, you, she tries to manipulate everyone. There main priority is the baby, to be honest they don't care much about her.'

'She's not well,' Danny pleaded.

'I know it's hard to accept, its cold. But that's the way it is. Are you still giving her money?'

'Sometimes'

'Stop. It could lead to all sorts of problems, accidents, over-doses, rape. Is she still up the camp?'

'I let her stay over mine a couple of times.'

'What? For God sake, what did I tell you? Don't get involved. I know there are strong feelings, but it's too dangerous. She needs to go home, she has family, children. She won't get the help here, she's not entitled. The council are not legally obliged to provide her with accommodation, there are other homeless pregnant women sleeping rough and they're not foreign. They also don't get into fights, steal from shops, take drugs and get arrested all the time. I have to go. I'll see what I can do, I'll talk to people. I promise I'll get back to you as soon as I can. Call me anytime, I'm working till ten.'

Danny felt a heavy hand on his shoulder. He turned around; it was a shock to see Yury standing behind him. They shook hands.

'How goes your life, Danny?'

'Good.'

'You haven't seen, Magda, have you?'

'No.'

'She took my money, she took my home, but I still love her, and I still want to be with her. Maybe I should go to the hospital, maybe I the crazy one. Did she give you sex when I was in prison?'

'No, I promise I-'

'She just wants your money for drugs. She doesn't care about you. She doesn't care about anyone except herself. She hasn't spoken to her children in six months, her sister told me. She told you her Mother and Father were dead, it's not true. Her father is in prison and her mother in an asylum.

'You spoke to her sister?'

'It's lies, all lies, huh why all the lies!'

Magda didn't talk much about her past. She told Danny her parents were both dead and her two daughters lived with her sister. Sometimes she changed the story. Sometimes her children were dead and sometimes they had been kidnapped by gypsies. She said she had another sister in America and one in Scotland, but sometimes it was one in Australia and one in Iceland.

'She doesn't know the truth, just uses people,' Yury continued.

'She says you beat her.'

'I hit her once, I make mistake. I was drunk, I'm sorry. She hit me all the time,' Yury pointed to different parts of his body scars and bumps. He pointed to a scar on his forehead 'She did this with a rock.' He pointed to a gap in his teeth, 'She knocked this tooth out with her foot,' he lifted his shirt up, turned around, and showed Danny a scar on his back. 'She slashes me with knife… It's important you have to know the truth. She took drugs in Lithuania; I didn't steal her passport or money. She stole my passport and money. She makes joke about peoples behind backs. Please don't give her any money, she just spends on drugs. She tells lies about people… Don't tell her anything. I know all your secrets about your past things you told her not to tell anyone. I know it's not your fault. I have to go… Business,' Yury bid farewell.

Magda wasn't waiting at the clocktower when Danny finished work, so he went straight home. When he arrived home, Magda was watching the television slumped in his armchair with half a bottle of vodka on her lap. She was on his phone.

'Hey, Carlos, what you doing? Come Danny's home, Seven Dover Street. Drink vodka. Come now! Sleep with my person, nice warm, not cold,' she slurred.

'Who are you calling?'

'Zip it,' she dialled again. 'Hey, baby, come Danny's place.' There was a knock at the door, 'one second,' she said. Magda put the phone down and answered the door. 'Surprise! Welcome Danny's place.'

A man and a woman in their twenties came in, loaded down with ruck sacks.   'Got any weed?'

She gave them both a big kiss and they came in.

'Relax, sit down, tv, shower,' she said. The two came in and walked around Danny's flat sheepishly.

'This where were staying?' said the girl.

Magda gave Danny a quick glance. 'Shh,' she replied.

'This your boyfriend?' she asked the girl. 'Thank you for bringing him, he's nice. Come my children, drink with me!' Magda poured out the girl some vodka.

'When you gonna tell me what we have to say?' She asked quietly, but not quietly enough.

'Shhh, later,' Magda looked guiltily at Danny.

'This is nice, thanks for letting us stay,' she talked in a fast and excitable manner, her accent a strange mix of English and Jamaican which constantly changed from one to the other. Her ginger braids looked like a basket of wriggling grass snakes on her head.

His long hair swept over his eyes. He shook and jittered about like he had a nervous twitch.

'You look a mess,' said Magda.

'I need to go wash myself and change,' said the man. He went into Danny's shower room while the other two sat down on Danny's bed, smoking, drinking and talking.

Danny felt strangely disconnected from all the strange unexpected behaviour, like it wasn't really happening. He had never been in this situation before and felt trapped. Danny was having the strangest thoughts.

'Don't look so worry, they nice people. I work with them packhouse,' said Magda.

Danny walked to the kitchen area and poured himself a glass of water. He stood there drinking and looking out the window across the roof tops of buildings, out over towards the cathedral. Then he heard a strange noise coming from the shower room, so he opened the door and saw the man sitting on the toilet about to stick a needle in his arm.

'What you looking at, you want a photo or something?'

'Get out get out now!'

'Cunt!'

'I knew it, I knew you had drugs.'

'Oh, don't piss your knickers love.'

Danny lifted him off the toilet seat and they stood nose to nose. He just smiled at him. Danny grabbed his jacket, twisted him around against the glass door and pushed him out. Then he heard a smash. He turned around and saw the girl kneeling on the floor, she had smashed her glass and spilt vodka everywhere. She just looked at him and started crying like a baby. Danny picked her up of the floor and put her back on the armchair.

'Go now!' Danny screamed. He went back to the man and saw piss dribbling down his trouser leg. 'Look at the fucking mess you're making,' all three were laughing at him. They were both pissed and stoned, easily manoeuvrable. Somehow, Danny managed to throw them both out the door and their ruck sacks out with them. 'Don't come back.'

Danny heard them walk down the steps and the door slam.

'Where they go?' Magda slurred. She spread out on the bed, blown out her head. Danny covered her with the duvet. 'Look, cosmetics for Joseph, no drugs, just vodka. Joseph more important.'

Danny lay down next to her and slept.

11

The park is busy today. As Danny sat on the park bench in the winter sunshine. The café has a queue of customers, mothers, toddlers, and school children chatting and playing football on their Christmas break. Its two o'clock now, and its chucking out time at the homeless shelter. Soon you will see them all shuffling and staggering through. The dealers won't be far behind. In fact, they are already here.

Drugs are sold, bought, and smoked openly in this park. It suffers from its location. Slap bang between the homeless centre, the police station, and the mental hospital. Subsequently, it's a magnet for every dealer, every addict, and every fruit loop in the city. Now the gangs are flooding in from London, taking advantage of the less sophisticated crackdowns than the capital.

There is a lot of fighting in this park. You've got travellers against each other, immigrants against each other, gangs against each other. So many feuds. There have been a few murders over the years, all drug related. In a city this size you probably have about a dozen people selling drugs at one level or another. It's a shame, the park looks so nice with its manicured lawns, flower beds, fountains, statues, and tree lined avenues.

Danny sat in the park with Magda, Sammy, and Ron, Magda's new best friend. He's pushing about seventy.

A chaotic mass of morbid, hateful, and unwanted thoughts raced around Danny's head like spaghetti junction. Danny slept okay, but he felt exhausted to the brink.

Shielding the sun from his eyes, he saw the unmistakeable figures of two of the biggest twats in town walking in unison. The tall thin one and his short chubby friend.

Nigel, otherwise known as Notas, and Brian, who called himself Hex, with their dopey German Shepherd. Nigel always dressed in black head to toe, with his long beard, and ponytail and mad staring eyes, he considered himself to be the self-proclaimed son of the devil. Hex was his cohort, and Hell the dog. They spotted them as they came walking towards them.

'Oh shit, its Notas,' said Sammy, worryingly. Notas always gave Sammy the heebie-jeebies.

'Oh no, not that twat,' Danny said.

'Quiet, he might hear you,' Sammy said, nervously.

'He's a pratt, he always has been. Always will be a massive pratt.'

'Shhh,' he's got the devil dog.

Danny nearly choked on his big mac. 'Devil dog, my arse, it's as soppy as the other two.'

'Shhh, quiet. They will hear you.'

The three of them came breezing over.

'Afternoon Nigel,' said Ron.

Ron seemed to keep dozing off momentarily and he had to keep picking up his cigarette and re lighting it. He had a big smile and a gormless expression on his face. He began tapping out a rhythm on his tobacco tin, then he blanked out again. Magda was smiling to herself behind her sunglasses, which she wore all year round. Ron woke up again, brushed ash of his chest and picked his cigarette back off the floor and relit it.

Nigel looked stony faced. He liked to exhibit an aura of evil, as he claimed he was the son of the devil. A lifetime of popping acid does that to you. He was pale as a sheet and as thin as a rake. He looked ridiculous in his huge sixteen-hole DMs, black drainpipe trousers, which made his legs look like pipe cleaners, and his long leather coat flapping in the wind. He tried to give Danny a terrifying stare, but he just looked pathetic.

'Piss of Nigel, we don't want any of your shit,' Danny said.

Hex spoke up in his high-pitched nasal whine. 'Do not disrespect Notas,' he said.

'Sorry N-o-t-a-s,' Danny replied, emphasising his stupid name.

'Magdalena, you look delectable as usual,' he said.

'Hey sweetie, you too thin. You should eat,' Magda replied.

Ron woke up again. 'You can't have any of our food, we paid for it,' said Ron, 'get your own, you can afford it.'

'I don't steal other people's food, just their souls.'

You had to laugh.

'What do you want, Nigel?'

'Did you notice how cold the park got when I came through the gate?' He said, in his slow, deep, and melodramatic voice.

'The suns just gone behind the clouds, that's all. Why are you so stupid, Nigel?'

'Shhh, don't say that. He's the devil's son,' whispered Sammy, nervously biting his fist.

'Devil's son, my arse,' Danny replied. Sammy was visibly intimidated.

'Spell it backwards,' said Hex.

'What?'

'Notas is Satan backwards.'

'No, it's not, it's sat on sat on,' said Ron.

Nigel looked perturbed.

The park was beginning to fill up. The usual idiots were shuffling through and a panda car was slowly cruising along the edge of the path. They were probably looking for someone. This was the first place they always looked.

'Magda, your taxis arrived,' Danny joked, looking at the Panda car.

'Huh, funny.'

Hell Dog, the soppiest looking dog around, started sniffing around their takeaway bags, so Danny fed it a hand full of fries.

'Do not feed the devil dog without permission,' said Hex.

'Devil dog?'

'Devil dog,' Hex knelt down and peeled back the ear off the dog. 'See, the sign of the devil.' Someone had written in black pen the numbers 666 on the inside of the dog's ear, you could see where the ink had smudged. 'See, the devil birth mark.' He glared at Danny, trying to freak him out. It was just pathetic.

'You did that with a pen,' Danny said, and fed the dog more chips. 'You need help.'

'We have to leave,' said Nigel. They watched them disappear, and like the son of the devil would, they stopped to buy candy canes.

It was warmer, but there was a chilly fresh breeze blowing and swinging the branches of the trees, which ran down a tidy path lined with park benches. There were lots of customers outside the café buying coffee and hotdogs, while it slowly pumped out soft Christmas classics to everybody waiting in line, laughing and enjoying themselves. There were lots of baby's in the park learning to walk. Danny watched them take a few steps, then tumble over.

Magda said that she felt her baby kick. Danny wasn't convinced, so he put his head to her stomach but all he could hear was gurgling sounds. Ron was on another planet.

'What you smoking, Ron, what's your favourite tobacco?' Danny asked.

'I ain't got one really, dunno what this is. Magda rolled it for me, nice and mellow,' Ron said, looking stoned.

Danny glanced at Magda; she was still smiling at something.

'Relax baby,' Magda slapped Ron on the thigh and Ron moved his hand between her legs. 'No,' Magda moved his hand away.

'Shame, you know you want it.'

'No.'

He tried again, 'I could satisfy your every need, I know how,' he went to kiss her on the mouth, but she turned her face away.

'No,' said Magda. He tried again. 'I said no, not here. People look me, no bitchy slag, stop.'

'Keep it up for hours.'

'Might stay up but nothing come out.'

'Why don't we test it out?'

'If you drop trousers I not tell if you man or woman, dick invisible need telescope,' said Magda.

'Don't you believe it,' he tried to kiss her again. Magda pushed him away.

'Relax, Ron, she doesn't want to kiss you, cut it out. Who do you think you are? You're old enough to be her grandad, you disgusting old git.'

'Fuck off!' shouted Ron, as he rubbed Magda's arse. Danny

stood up and Magda moved away from Ron looking annoyed.

The kids from the college were playing football. A young lad miss hit the ball and it came flying towards them, hit Danny on the head and then bounced onto Magda.

Magda bolted up. She was hot with sweat, wild eyed, and had a look of fury.

'What you doing dickhead! Woman pregnant!' Magda continued, 'what is this dickhead wanky!'

The lad was terrified. 'S-so sorry,' he stuttered quietly and feebly.

Magda cursed him. Her words full of venom and wrath. 'I kill your person. I promise you dead!'

She never saw him trembling or heard him sobbing after Danny threw the ball back.

'Just calm down,' said Danny, as he rubbed her back and arm.

She managed to pull herself together.

A group of Somalis were in the park sitting high up on the bank like a pack of hyenas stalking a victim or on the lookout for potential customers. They thought the whole thing was very funny. They were all in their twenties. Sometimes Danny could see them eyeing up the young teenage girls and on occasions they would approach them and start chatting them up. The girls didn't like it very much and Danny often wondered if there was something far more sinister going on.

The kids on their bikes arrived with the orders and the woman with the pram who hides the wraps under the baby. Danny walked over to the café in the park.

Jamie was standing outside the café selling the big issue, but it always sounded like he was asking for a big tissue. 'Big tissue, big tissue please,' he would say. Some people must have thought that he was suffering from a permanent cold.

Monday, the first day the new weekly issue came out, was always the best payday. This week the issue had a picture of a big ginger tom cat on the front cover. A street cat named Bob. It looked like it was selling fast.

'How is it going,' Danny asked him.

'Not bad, only been here a few hours but I think the reason its selling so quick is because it's got a picture of a soppy cat on the front cover.'

'Have you seen the film?'

'No.'

'Have you read the book?'

'A bit of it.'

'What you think?'

'It's a nice enough story, not very realistic though.'

'Well it's for kids, they probably only bought it because they liked the cover.'

'People like soppy cats, the internet is full of videos of soppy cats which get millions of hits. People love cats.'

A woman interrupted their conversation and bought a copy of the magazine.

'It must be true,' said Danny.

'Fair enough. You can't really tell the truth. Nobody wants to watch a film or read a book about some poor sod shitting himself or getting the crap kicked out of him in a public toilet. Nobody wants to know about some kid selling his arse for a packet of weed and waking up with his face in a puddle of sick.

Jamie was a bit camp in his mannerisms. Danny thought that it must have been the artist in him. Danny gave him a pound and went on his way.

Danny went back over to the others sitting on the bench.

Ron put his hand on Magda's knee. Magda touched Ron's chest.

'Ronnie, please, some money for car boot tomorrow. I buy you nice jacket.'

Ron put his hand in his pocket, got out his wallet, and gave her one hundred notes and a kiss.

'Thanks, love you baby,' she kissed him back slowly on the lips. 'Five minutes.' Magda stood up abruptly and just left them and started walking off in the direction of the band stand.

All the arseholes were sitting there together, telling lies to one another and placing each other on pedestals, ready and waiting only to strike them down once their backs were turned. Danny watched her walk up to Aaron and they made an exchange. Then she didn't come back, she just carried on walking in the opposite direction towards the west side of the park. Once again, Danny was compelled to follow her, and he walked right up to the bandstand.

'We never gave her any weed,' said Aaron.

'She's not right for God's sake.'

'What you going to do about it?' Aaron replied, as he put his hands-on Danny's shoulders.

Danny said nothing.

'Ah, go pick up some fag butts,' said Bobby, Billy's younger brother, who was trying to step out of his older brothers shadow and make a name for himself.

'Would you like a job?' Asked Bobby.

'What?'

'Sales.'

'Oh, Jesus.'

'You make more money in one day than you would in a week.'

'What?'

'You heard.'

'I'm sure, Dimitri, could fix you up. Everyone knows you, trusts you.'

'I will think about it.'

Danny needed the toilet. There was one in the park. There was another person in there when he went in. Danny stood a comfortable distance from him and relieved himself.

As Danny was urinating, he noticed him looking at him. So, Danny glared at him and he looked away. He was a youngster, about thirteen, and Danny had never seen him before in his life. He was kind of scary looking but stupid at the same time. And he was bombed out of his skull on something. He had a pale white face and his eyes were blacked up with mascara. He looked like a reject from the land of the living dead. It was a shock at first.

'Got any weed?' He said.

'No,' said Danny.

'Got anything else?'

'No.'

Danny continued to relieve himself, but the kid was staring at his privates and then he stroked Danny's backside.

'Fuck off!' Danny yelled. The kid just smiled. 'I'm not interested!' Danny told him as he pulled up his trousers and did his flies up.

Danny went to side-step him, but the kid blocked his path.

Danny went to walk the other way, but the kid blocked his path. Danny just stood opposite him and stared at him for five seconds. He was weird. The kid just smiled. In the old days, you would have described him as a goth.

'What you want, money?'

Danny was annoyed. Then the kid just pushed himself against Danny and pressed his hand hard against his privates, squeezing Danny's balls.

Danny stood there, frozen. He didn't know what to do. Now there was a lot of concern flying around. Danny was concerned about what he was going to do next. The kid was concerned about what Danny was going to do next. But no one was more concerned than the elderly gentleman who came in to use the toilet saw them both standing in front of the urinals with his hand clutching Danny's balls, and began walking backwards apologetically.

Danny grabbed the kids arms and managed to twist him around and push him out of the toilet. The kid tumbled over the steps and fell over himself onto the ground.

Danny noticed an AA poster pinned to the trunk of an old tree, still inside its plastic weatherproof covering. It showed a picture of a man curled up inside a giant bottle of beer like a prisoner, no doubt it was nailed to the tree by some person who means well, as source of encouragement and motivation to the park's scallywags. Danny had to laugh. The message, it seemed, hadn't exactly got through the thick sculls of the drunks in this park.

A brave and brazen schoolgirl walked past him wearing a t-shirt with the slogan, 'Normal people scare me.' It was a popular t shirt these days.

The girl, bless her, probably had a few minor mental health issues to contend with. But she couldn't compete in their league. Yet, they weren't normal people, so they probably didn't scare her. None of them showed any signs of behaviour of being normal. In fact, they showed no signs at all that they might actually be human beings. It took about a week of the booze before anyone showed any signs at all they might be normal, and even then, the signs were few. This park was worse than the nut house.

Danny stood outside the toilet block and waited just in case Magda returned. The local numpties were back, and it wasn't long before the party in the park was in full swing.

Everybody swapped stories and they all told each other lies about the money they had. They begged and conned the amount of whiskey they drunk, and the amount dope they smoked.

Danny could see a motley crew from where he stood and watched the drunks piss all over the flower beds and all over the grass. Some of them walked around in the park talking to themselves all day like zombies, walking around in circles and asking people for money. They were prone to shaking fits and smashing their heads on the ground. Others were frozen like statues, high on spice. No one took any notice. After a while, you didn't care. Anyone who had the misfortune to have a fit was always minus their money or gear when they came around.

Two of the girls came out of the toilet and waddled over to Danny, dressed in a tight-fitting dresses and blouse. One of them looked attractive from a distance, but close up and personal in the cold light of day he saw her broken nose and the scar on her face. The other girl's nose was broken as well, flat against her face like a mushroom. They sat down on the bench next to the strangest of creatures.

His face was covered in bumps and scratches. He wore a dress, high heeled shoes and torn tights. He was telling everybody that it was his time of the month and described all the gory details in glorious technicolour, explicit in his descriptions about the amount of blood and how his doctor was going to prescribe him oestrogen.

He was a very damaged human being who had suffered in his life at the hands of his father and two uncles with the most horrendous forms of abuse you could imagine. A physical, mental, and sexual a psychiatrist's nightmare. Nobody liked him, but they tolerated him. Pitied him, really. He stayed with them for protection, sharing the money he got by selling himself in the toilet to weirdos for five pound a blow tragic case.

Over in the far corner of the park, Spencer hid in the bushes like a snipper paparazzi with his thirty times zoom lens and twenty million pickles. He zoomed in on the small group of drunks, fooling about around the bench screaming and jumping on each other's backs, on the other side of the park.

While all this was going on, Spencer was slowly making his way closer to the group, occasionally dropping to one knee and firing off a few shots of the ducks on the river. The group hadn't taken much notice of him up to now, having left him relatively alone. But he was slowly edging himself precariously closer. His editor had always told him to feel the fear and do it anyway, risking life and limb for that perfect shot, until he caught the attention of a member of the group who gave him the v sign. Un perturbed, he made his way foolishly closer.

'Nice equipment. Is that a Nikon?' Danny asked.

'Canon actually.'

'Taken any good snaps?'

'Take a picture of this darling.' A woman turned her back on him, lowered her trousers, pulled down her knickers, and mooned him as the other all cackled and roared.

'Fucking cunt snapper,' someone said.

'You want a close up, how about a full-frontal beaver shot?' She squealed.

'Do you mind if I take your photos, it's for a book I'm doing?'

'Cost ye.'

'How much?'

'Fifty.'

'How about twenty?'

'Done.'

He began to fire of the shots in rapid succession, like he was at a photo shoot on location somewhere exotic. He beamed widely as the women postured and blew kisses at him.

After he had finished snapping, Clara, the tallest and best looking of the group, sauntered towards him slowly. She pressed her finger into the middle of his chest, slowly ran it down towards his navel, blew into his ear and then, in a low and seductive voice, she propositioned him.

'If you're interested,' she said.

'Interested,' Spencer gulped. 'Let's get away from these boring bastards, I'd much rather spend time with you.'

Spencer showed his true colours. Stepping over an old drunk lying on the steps, she looked loaded as she led him down to the dark cell, through the toilets and into small cramped room.

Inside that dimly lit room with her back towards him, she

dropped to her knees and hoisted up her dress to reveal her curvaceous thighs and great big moon of a derriere. Spencer felt faint and leered at her intensely as he fired of a couple of shots. He moved up closer behind her and kissed the back of her neck, then on to the ears, shoulders, then down her arms, and then slowly worked his way down her spine. Spencer felt things stir in his lower regions, so he removed his trousers.

Spencer felt her sweet-smelling body as he gently squeezed his manhood between her legs. It was tight. His body spasmed as he pushed and coursed the ninety-degree struggle. Rolling and writhing on top of her, inside her cramped space, inside that cramped space, in extasy, slowly meeting a climax, throbbing inside her, and pumping hard until he ejaculated.

She pulled out and slowly turned towards Spencer. He removed his curly wig from his head, then threw away his dress from his body and bared his hairy chest. Further down, he revealed his terrible secret as he stood before Spencer with his big part swinging between his legs.

Spencer was full of the fear of god and gaped in sheer terror. Cold shivers raced down Spencer's spine and his whole body just seemed to drain of life. For a few seconds he was paralysed with fear and couldn't move. Quickly, he scrabbled about on all fours trying to gather up his clothes and he tried to dress but he was in a total state of panic. He was so shocked that he tried to put his legs through his shirt sleeves and arms through his trousers realising his predicament.

Spencer was trapped and couldn't seem to find the door or co-ordinate his movements, so he ran around the confined space like a frightened rat. He crashed through the door and ran screaming up the steps before hurtling arse over elbow outside, barefoot clutching hold of his shoes, trousers and precious camera in his arms.

Danny looked on, as passers-by and people gathered around him to see what was happening. But Danny didn't have time to stop and stare as he had more pressing engagements, and so he just watched poor Spencer run out of the park half naked holding onto his possessions for dear life.

12

Danny was sweeping near the clocktower bench when he spotted something. On first impressions it looked like a tea bag, so he held it up so he could see it more clearly. It was about the size of a tea bag. A brown powdery substance in a muslin package, broken at one end. He took it over to Stellica who was sitting on the bench and showed it to him.

'Do you know what this is?' Danny asked Stellica, who glanced at it then studied it more closely.

'Heroin.'

'You sure?'

'Yes, I been on the streets long enough to recognise this shit.'

'I thought it was white?'

'If its brown powder raw, cook it up white, take your pick.'

Danny walked a bit further along, then put it in his front pocket, lent against the wall and radioed control.

'Danny to control,' he said.

'Go ahead.'

'I've found a packet of heroin, what should I do with it?'

'Bring it up stairs for now. Where abouts did you find it?'

'Clocktower.'

'Bring it up.'

'Understood. Over.'

Upstairs in the control room, Ted sat staring at a wall of monitors. One hundred and fifty cameras which covered the shopping centre and received live feeds from other cameras across the city. Danny gave him the packet.

'It's not a tea bag,' he said.

Ted sniffed it, held it up to the light, then wrapped it up in a small packet, labelled it, and put it in the draw. 'Cheers mate I'll smoke it later,' he replied, then zoomed in on one of the cameras to a woman sitting on the bench beside the clocktower. 'Your friend,' he continued, 'when's the baby due?'

Danny took a closer look and saw Magda. 'Any second.'

'Bet it's a girl. She still in that tent?'

'Yes.'

'You still sleep in the tent sometimes?'

'Sometimes.'

'Be careful mate,' said Ted.

'She can't stop smoking cannabis and it's fucked her brain up big time. She thinks the father is Prince Harry and thinks her grandads Adolf Hitler'

'Mmm.'

'She needs help. It's not fair. She's a human being, she shouldn't have to live like that.'

'Just be careful, it's not just her is it, it's all those other nutters she knocks about with.'

Danny chatted with Ted for a while before he knocked off. Ted needed a break from looking at the cameras. Danny asked him what the funniest thing he had ever seen was. He said most of the fun happens at night and told Danny a few funny stories.

Danny left the control room. It was time to go home. The moment he stepped outside the wind picked up rattling the

Christmas lights, and a thick blanket of grey cloud slowly crept up covering the sky. The rain began to gently fall. A flash of dirty yellow lit up the cloud and the thunder rumbled like God breaking wind. Twenty seconds later, the clouds parted, and the sun came out. The birds sang and he saw himself reflected in the puddles. He walked through the square and headed towards the clocktower.

When Magda saw Danny, she jumped up and didn't stop kissing him. She wouldn't stop kissing him until she spotted someone else.

'Look, Fernando! Hey, Fernando!' Magda shouted.

Fernando was a test driver for the mobility centre. Every day you could see him cruising around the town on the latest mobility scooters. He was Italian and in his younger days he was a charmer, a real lady's man - so he said. Now, all the old dears loved him and flirted with him. He looked like a professor with his small John Lennon glasses, long white bushy beard, and swept back hair. He was just coming out of the Tesco Express when they saw him.

Magda ran over to him, flung her arms around him, and smothered his face in a rapid succession of kisses.

'This is a wonderful girl,' he said.

'She's a nightmare,' said Danny.

'Look at the beautiful dresses you buy me,' Magda said, as she proceeded to look inside the bag. She started to unpack the garments, then unfold them and display them for the men. 'Dresses white, black, red, and sexy knickers,' she giggled.

'This is a present for a ma wife, two hundred a pounds this cost me,' Fernando panted, as he was shivering from the cold.

Magda sighed.

'No,' Magda grabbed him by the arm and took behind a coffee and donut stall, out of Danny's sight.

'I can't a talk for long I'm with my wife,' said Fernando.

His wife was hanging around. She looked like a bulldog chewing a wasp. She was a large lady with a fierce Italian temperament.

Fernando looked around nervously and they went around the side of the shop, clutching each other tightly. Danny watched from a distance. She didn't let go of his arm and kept rubbing his back vigorously. Danny couldn't hear what they were talking about, but he did see him reach into his back pocket, take out his wallet, and then give her sixty pounds.

Magda pulled herself close to Fernando and with her usual husky whisper in his ear she said, 'Fernando, please, some more money for tobacco?'

'Ask, Danny.'

'No, he no more money. Please, just ten pounds?'

'I haven't got anymore.'

Magda's face flashed rage for a few seconds.

'Please, ten pounds. No drugs, I stop drugs. Please you know me no liar. Ten, please, maybe twenty?'

'No,' he said firmly.

'Please, I buy present for Danny. It's his birthday.'

'Later.'

Her face flashed anger momentarily. Sometimes it was like she had this underlying rage that turned on and off when she didn't get her way. She had trouble containing it.

'No, now!'

'I'm not a footballer, I'm not a millionaire,' he reached into his pocket again and put more money into her pocket again.

Magda gave him a big hug and kiss and bolted, leaving him standing all by himself.

'One second, pee pee,' she shouted.

Billy was hiding around the back of the public toilets near the salvation army. He was in charge of his own crew of dealers. He was always with his pet gorilla, Aaron. You could see them at the station in the morning, the park in the afternoon, and outside the toilets in the evening.

Billy always had Aaron with him, a burly scary looking ginger haired ape who always wore a white vest and cap, whatever the weather. They were travellers with a nasty reputation for violence and they worked for the Albanians. They sold drugs and they took drugs as well. People knew to keep their distance.

Magda went around the back of the toilets and scored, then disappeared inside the ladies.

Danny went to look for Magda and bumped into Fernando.

'Where's Magda gone,' he asked Fernando.

'Toilet.'

'Had a good day?'

'I'm gonna ask a Magda to marry me, live with me. First have to tell the wife to bugger off.'

'Are you crazy?'

'We love each other.'

'She loves your money.'

'We enjoy each other's company. I ask a her, do you a love me? She says, ah yes as I do her.'

'What about Yury?'

'She doesn't love Yury. Basta punch her, she's a gonna leave Yury, come a live with me. I'm a gonna look after the lady, get her of the funny cigarettes. She a need's a good man to a take care of a her.'

Heading through the throng, Danny could see Fernando's wife moving towards them from a distance. Danny began to hum the theme tune from jaws. Fernando turned around, sharp.

'Oh, fuck, it's the wife!'

She screamed a high-pitched whine. It sounded more like a cat screeching than a person. When she spoke, it was very hard to decipher. She came right up to them.

'What ah you doing with that woman!'

'What woman?'

'I a see her!'

His wife was scary and mean, built like a rhino with flaming nostrils.

'You fucking her!' She was balling, crying, swearing and hollering. 'I hate ah you! Ungrateful bastard, you still my husband!'

Then she started screaming, wailing and whacking him around the head hard with her umbrella. Fernando covered his head with his hands, shielding himself from the blows.

'Why don't you a love me anymore!'

His wife grabbed him by the arm and nearly dragged him of his feet as she bundled him away and pushed him into a taxi, leaving Danny all by himself with Magda, who was nowhere to be seen. Danny shouted as loud as he could into the female toilet, but all he heard was his own echo. Then he saw Billy and Aaron standing around the corner, so he marched up to them.

'Where's Magda?' He demanded.

'No idea,' said Billy.

'Did you give her anything?'

'What do you care?'

'She's about to drop for fucks sake!'

'We never gave her any weed,' said Aaron.

'Something spicy,' Billy said.

Aaron put his hands onto Danny's shoulders, 'what you going to do about it?'

They just stared. Danny said nothing. Then.

'Go fuck yourself Aaron'

Aarons eyes flickered, then he grinned his famous rotten toothed grin, and glared right at Danny. He felt paralysed with fear. This was Aaron, after all. What a stupid thing to say.

Smack!

His head met Danny's head and he felt a crack against his skull, then an immense pain and everything imploded. The next thing he knew he had a crunching headache, he was lying on the ground beneath them, and they were all standing over him, looking down. Danny staggered to his feet, dazed.

'Leave him, he's not worth the hassle,' said Billy.

Danny staggered into the toilets, dripping blood all along the pavement and toilet floor. He saw his reflexion appear in the cracked mirrors above the sinks. Bloodshot tired eyes set in, his face was as pale as a ghost with bumps and grazes from previous outings. He had a bad cut to his head.

'Hello, can you hear me, is anyone in there?' Danny said to himself. Then, in a confused state, he went into a cubicle and proceeded to wrap half a roll of toilet paper around his head like a turban, to stem the flow of blood.

There was a loud thump at the door.

'Hold on,' Danny unlocked the door and fell outside. He tried to pull himself up of the floor, using a sink for leverage, but fell backwards into a wastepaper bin, totally dazed and disorientated. The man grabbed his arms and steadied him to his feet.

'Thank you, sir,' he said, as he escorted him outside. Danny hobbled down the path in the direction of the west park, bleary eyed and puffy faced with the wind blowing right through him. The toilet paper on his head slowly began to unravel as he shuffled across the road bridge, over the one-way system, cars and lorries thundering bellow him.

Danny went to the west park to try and find her but all he could find were the usual idiots hanging around the Italian war memorial, getting pissed and smoking weed. A couple was there with their two children. The father - smashed out his skull on special brew. The mother - smoking a joint as the two children sat quietly talking to each other. The younger girl was colouring in a picture and the older brother was doing his homework.

'Have any of you seen, Magda?' Danny asked.

'No, if you see her tell her I've got something for her,' said the father, then the mother started to perform what looked like an unusual red Indian rain dance, whooping like a Cherokee and stamping her feet. They paid no attention to the way Danny looked. Abnormal is normal, in an abnormal world.

An hour before dusk fell, stillness was in the air. Not a bird, not a snapping twig. The sun was starting to drain the light on the world.

Danny heard the neighing of a horse. He looked behind him and saw a large grey stallion by the edge of a fence. It was black and white with its mane falling wildly across its nose and eyes. He stepped over the barbed wire and into the pasture where it had been grazing all day on thrown out bales of hay and quenching its first from a rusty old water trough. He walked over to it, ripped up a handful of long hay, fed it, and patted it, stroking its neck which it shook vigorously before trotting away. Danny felt tired so he sat down on a mound of earth to catch his breath. He began to contemplate things. A mangey looking mongrel came sniffing towards him, then started to claw at the earth with its paws, throwing up great clumps under its feet. Danny's legs were getting pelted as it dug away. Then it stopped digging and started sniffing at the ground, then commenced to dig further down. It clawed deeper and deeper.

It was getting darker, and a chill was in the air. The dog's owner came over and tried to pull the dog away with its lead, but it started digging harder earth. Stones, bits of brick and gravel began flying everywhere. Danny was trying to shield himself as much as possible as he was getting bits of earth in his eyes and in his mouth, trying to spit it out.

The dog stopped digging and the old man saw something sticking out of the earth. It looked like a small bone or stick. Then the dog tore it from the earth and ran into the bushes with its owner yelling after it.

After searching around the park for hours, asking around, Danny eventually found Magda, by herself at the far end of the park.

There was a strange solitude and silence that possessed that quiet secluded corner. High up, the setting sun cast its final rays over them as she stood in front of him, shrouded in an incredible white light. She took a drag and seemed in a very relaxed state. She pulled out her hair band tossed her hair back, kicked off her shoes, and groaned pleasantly. She paced around in a circle, bare foot through the shallow puddles of melting snow, kicking it up from the surface. Her feet and ankles were covered in ice. She rolled her head around and screeched with delight, then clapped her hands above her head as if trying to catch imaginary flying insects. She was kicking up snow, clapping and waving her arms in front of her, swatting at the imaginary butterflies, screeching, and walking around in circles.

It confused him and bewildered him. It terrified him inside. She walked around the empty corner of the park as Danny sat on the steps of a fountain, watching her carefully taking a drag, laughing, and stumbling. She was a little uneasy on her feet. Her voice was slurring and rambled along a disordered and incoherent babbling.

'Danny, wakey, wakey, baby!' Magda whooped and screamed, 'you know I love you, baby!'

There was a beautiful golden sun on the horizon, just about to set. Danny looked down at her bag which she had left next to the fountain and saw a black empty packet next to it.

His heart sank upon the sight of her in the distance. As she suddenly collapsed. Danny ran over to her and dropped to his knees beside her.

Magda clutched her stomach and groaned, 'oh, pain, help me!'

'What's wrong, is it the baby?'

'No. I don't know.'

She started panting heavily, then fitting and drooling from her mouth. Danny sat there, helplessly; he was panic stricken. Then her body went limp and lifeless, but she was still breathing. Then he remembered what to do and he put her into the recovery position. First, he checked inside her mouth to make sure she was still breathing. She was. It's not unusual for someone to swallow their tongue and choke to death during in a fit. She was heavy.

A community warden walked past on a routine patrol, by the grace of God.

'Shit is that Magda?' she got out her radio and spoke in a calm manner. 'PAPA 127. Urgent assistance required. Pregnant female fitting. Looks like Magda, west park near water fountain.'

All Danny could do was sit and hold her hand.

'OK, ambulance is on its way. Do you know what she's taken?'

Danny held her hand tightly, she dug her nails into his palm then her body went weak and she let go of his hand. 'What should we do?' Danny cried.

'It's OK, ambulance is on its way.'

'I think she took this,' Danny picked up the discarded packet and gave it to the warden. She looked at the packet briefly and sighed.

13

The Christmas lights shone like blue and white icicles, swinging in the wind, strung between the buildings either side of the high street, above the Christmas market. The lights were good this year. Giant blue, white and red snowflakes sparkled and flashed with globe shaped lights wrapped with golden flashing bulbs.

Danny couldn't tell what he was supposed to be dressed up like. Tigger in a tiger onesie, jumping up and down in time with the perpetual thumping beat of the beat box, littered with expletives blaring out at full volume camped in the doorway of Marks and Spencer's, passing shoppers throwing coppers into his cap. It wasn't long before the enforcement officer took out his walkie talkie and approached him, just as the manager of Marks and Spencer's came outside and an argument erupted between the three.

Further down the street, a smart looking woman with tight fitting jeans and a black pull over was walking around with her laminated postcards. It was of a child in a hospital bed with all manner of tubes and pipes sticking out of her and attached to a heart monitor. She claimed it was her sick child and she needed to raise money for a private operation heart transplant in America.

Everybody, giving, giving, giving. No wonder they never left this place. Everything was a scam, a con manipulation.

The Afghans had parked their bicycles outside Mc Donald's restaurant and were sitting on top of their Deliveroo and Uber boxes, playing with their iPhone's. They were waiting for their orders to be made up so they could peddle them off a hundred yards up the street to the lazy bastards who couldn't be bothered to walk the hundred steps outside there flats to get it themselves.

The old boys on their mobility scooters were huddled together under the awning talking about the good old days.

Further up the high street, Danny sat on the bench near the park. The traffic was heavy streaming in all directions. Through a gap in the traffic, he saw Marta outside West Park Towers with her ruck sack of sandwiches and flasks of tea. He stood up and shouted across to her, but she didn't hear him. So, Danny got up and when the lights turned green he ran across to the other side of the street.

'Where are you going?' Danny asked.

'The camp behind the park,' she replied.

'You're walking through the park, be careful.'

'God will protect me.'

'I'm coming with you.'

They walked through the park gates and watched a group of four teenagers all hanging onto one swing, being pushed by a couple of others. Back and forth they swung like a pendulum, the metal chains grinding and staining under their weight sounded like the metallic wheezing of a chronic asthmatic, which groaned in time with the creaking of the overburdened seesaw. Everything needed a good oiling. Kids span around and around on the roundabout, then jumped off, some falling over, and others landing on both feet then staggering around like old drunks. Along the edge of the river, Danny watched a yellow football floating downstream on the current and saw another group of teenagers wrapping a swing around the overhead bar by its chains so the little kids couldn't reach them.

'Why do you believe in God? You look too clever to believe in that crap.'

'Don't you?' Marta asked, rather taken back by his question.

'There are a few ideas I can't get my head around.'

'But you're so kind.'

'Explain to me the emasculate conception.'

She looked dumbstruck, scratched her head and racked her brains for an answer, but couldn't think of anything worthy of an answer.

'Walking on water, loaves and fishes, rising from the dead,' he continued to ask, and she continued to look puzzled.

'But he was the son of God,' she finally replied.

'Possibly. Personally, I think the bible is just a big fairy tale. All religions have them. But the bible is the world's biggest selling fairy tale. Bigger than Harry Potter.'

She looked flabbergasted.

'OK, so who do you think made the universe?'

'I'm a big bang theorist,' replied Danny.

'Yes, but what was in the beginning. It says in Genesis, in the beginning there was a word and the word.'

'Man made God; God didn't make man.'

'Please stop.'

Marta was a good person, but she needed to explain the unexplainable.

'Just because you can't feel hear or see something, doesn't mean it doesn't exist. What about electricity, we all know it exists, but most people can't see or explain it.'

'You can feel an electric shock though.'

'This is true.'

'No scientist will ever discover God.'

'Please. Look up into the sky at night ask yourself, how? There are so many things you can't explain in life. So many things you aren't meant to understand. The fact is, he exists in so many people's hearts, all over the world, giving hope where there is no hope, and strength to help people overcome hardship. We all need something to believe in.'

She was right, of course. And despite their differences, she didn't preach or try to convert. They were near the fountain when they heard shouting.

One man ran forward with all his gust from inside the toilet and jumped three foot into the air, flying over the bench and landing the other side. He then stumbled headfirst into the toilet door and the crowd screamed. Then came another from outside, he flew into the air, caught the back of the bench with his feet and came crashing down in a crumpled heap to the ground. Before he could get to his feet, out came another through the toilet door, followed by another, then another. They were coming from all directions, jumping over the bench and missing each other by inches like a drunken aerial display team. They started slamming into the bench, into the bushes, into the toilet doors, and into each other, like Kamikaze crashing on top and into the surrounding crowd. It was a riot.

One man smacked right into a much larger man mid-flight, coming from the opposite direction and got knocked right on top of the bench and came crashing and smashing to the ground. He managed to stagger up, but he had a cut head, blood was seeping down his face and all over his shirt as he glared right at Danny. He swayed from side to side, picked up a drink and said, 'fun here tonight, isn't it.'

Then another flew past them, crashing into the bench. Another flew right over the bench; everyone was crashing into everyone else and there was smashed glass and blood all over the bench and grass. Then people started pulling each other off the ground, urging them to have another go, but they were staying put. But they wouldn't give up, determined to make them jump again. So, they got up and ran with all there might, and jumped. One cleared the stall, clashing heads with another, and fell arse over elbow. The crowd was ecstatic, waving their arms about in the air, yelling and screaming, clutching hold of their vodka bottles. A bunch of lunatics' sky-high on the adrenalin, rush jumping up and down in the air, crashing down on top of each other and smashing the empties, spraying fragments of glass everywhere.

A very heavy-set man, uneasy on his feet, staggered through the crowd, bidding each and every person along the way. He hovered as he reached Danny and nearly knocked him over.

'Sorry Laddie,' he muttered and then he stood at the front of the bench, with beer stains running down his chest and trousers. Then, a woman came walking towards him, dressed in black. She tried to walk past him, but he deliberately blocked her path. Then he made a grope for her and pushed her against the wall. She screamed. Then all hell broke loose.

Someone grabbed Danny. They hurriedly dragged him away from the crowd as the game of bench jumping was abandoned into an all-out brawl, with bottles being thrown over the bench instead of people.

You could hear the sound of barking dogs. The sound growing ever louder around them. Through the trees, Danny saw a dog tearing across the park towards him. He thought in no time at all he would be savaged to death but then it disappeared from view into the bushes. Suddenly everyone stopped. The others got out of their tents and started looking around nervously. Then Danny spotted it between the trees and pointed it out. Tadious, the biggest of the group, went into his tent and emerged with a large knife. Martin went to his and got a big lump of wood.

Out of the trees at the edge of the park they raised up and charged forwards. Dozens of them. All dressed in combats and ski masks, firing sticks, bricks, and stones. Hurling them at the group. Throwing more of their ammunition from rucksacks. The others ran into their tents and got weapons.

Two tried to pull Danny off somewhere but they were beaten away by Martin who defended him with a wooden club. Danny was unarmed and stuck in the middle of it all.

Then Danny heard a scream, he turned fast to see that one thug had pushed Marta over. She was kicking and lashing out at his lower body. Another jumped on her. They were going to pound her brains in. Danny had to do something. He picked up a discarded bat, charged towards them like a barbarian, then cracked it over one of the attacker's shoulders and kicked the other in the back of the head. They rolled off. Marta ran like the wind.

Danny was plunged into complete darkness. He heard a muffled scream as he disappeared under the surface. Freezing water filled his lungs, choking him of breath. He felt his heart press against his ribcage. He felt his heart pumping hard filling him with adrenalin. He was drowning. He reached out blindly gasping as the chill stole his final breaths. His whole body became numb and useless and his life flashed before his eyes.

Danny grabbed hold of a leg, then a waist, then an arm. Someone was pulling him up, but the intense cold had sapped all of his strength.

The next thing he remembered someone was sticking their fingers down his throat, then turning him on his side. He was coughing up a length of green plant life.

Someone had managed to drag him out of the fountain. They sat looking at each other, dripping wet and shivering.

14

Christmas day.

Danny could see her through the glass window of the special baby unit. She was sitting with her back to him, next to the cot. Danny was shown in after he removed his coat and thoroughly disinfected his hands. Danny went in and looked in the cot, but he couldn't see anything. Then he glanced at Magda and she had the tiniest bundle in her arms. A four-hour old wrinkled little face.

'Hello, Danny, this is my son. Danny, meet, Danny.'

Niagara Falls. Tears streamed down his face. He gulped and spluttered. He couldn't contain his emotions.

'Happy birthday, Danny, welcome to the world,' Danny gulped.

'I hope they're tears of joy,' said the nurse. 'We have a grading system for all new-born babies in this hospital and Danny gets full marks, ten out of ten. A perfect little boy.'

'Ten out of ten. You're beautiful,' Danny said.

'My baby big, my baby eight pounds,' said Magda.

'I'll give you ten.'

'Ha, Danny, not for sale.'

Magda had to have an emergency caesarean otherwise she could have lost the baby. But Magda's social worker and interpreter were standing close to them looking at all the other babies in the unit who were considered special measures or at risk. Danny Kissed Magda on the head. It was a relief and a miracle the baby was okay. Everything he did over the past year to keep them both alive had worked.

'I love you, Magda. Danny too.'

'I know, one hundred percent.'

'Magda, you have five minutes, then you have to talk to Rachel,' said the nurse.

'Danny come too,' Danny looked at Rachel, she nodded.

They wheeled Magda through to a small room. Danny sat on a chair and held Magda's hand, still crying. Rachel, her social worker, and Petra, the interpreter, sat in front of them.

Rachel started to speak to Magda about how she was feeling about the future of her children and what they had discussed in previous sessions. The interpreter spoke when it got too complicated. Sometimes it felt like an interrogation, but Magda was calm under the pressure. Danny told her not to get angry no matter what was said. He told her to show them how nice and kind you can be, show them you're a good person, a fit mother. But they knew she wasn't right in the head. It was like a giant elephant squirting water in the room. Then the conversation got more heated.

'Magda, you have had four abortions in the past four years. Four have been up to the maximum term allowed, have you ever heard of contraception?'

'No, me no contraception. Me a catholic. No contraception.'

'I didn't think the catholic church agreed with abortion either, isn't it banned in your country?'

Magda was silent.

'You have repeatedly turned down all our offers of help. Your sister tells us you haven't spoken to your children in nearly two years.'

'Lies, lies.'

'Do you have trouble bonding with your children?'

'I love my children! Please just quickly job home, my children can stay with me here England.'

'Why have you not spoken to them in two years?'

'I get job in packhouse quickly, I get contract.'

'Your sister thinks you're an unfit mother.'

'Bullshit! My sister never says this.'

'What is more important, Magda, drink drugs or your children?'

'Little Joseph, little Danny, my daughters, Anna, Maria! I stop drink drugs, I promise no more. Finish. I spend money on Joseph now.'

'You have no money, how?'

'I don't know I get job quickly, I change, please, no take my Joseph. You no take my, Danny, I his mother, he my son. No, I stop everything now, I stop I promise.'

'You have to prove to us that you can stop.'

'I have nothing, why you hate me. You not my friend, why you all hate me!'

'We offered you a specialist mother and baby unit in London with round the clock help and support. When you had Joseph, we offered you housing in various places, but you turned them down. We try to help you, but you keep turning us down. You have repeatedly turned down our offers of help, you refused to speak to us when we came to the centre looking for you, and you are always late for meetings.'

'He's not your son, he's my son.'

'Do you know who Danny's father is?'

'His father not important.'

'Do you know who the father of Joseph is, how many sexual partners have you had in the past year, how many?'

'I pregnant.'

'You're always pregnant. I have a report from probation. You have been arrested this year six times for public order offences. Drunk and disorderly, affray, criminal damage, assault, assault on police officers, theft, arson. You even stole your child from the foster parents when they came to visit. You said in court, I quote, 'I like fight, I like drink, I like cause trouble!' Do you think you have a drink problem, how much marijuana do you smoke?'

'Just little.'

'We will conduct tests. You will be tested monthly for use of all illegal substances from now on. You will be given three months to find yourself suitable accommodation and suitable employment. You must remain clean for three months, then we will review your situation. You must not get into any more trouble with the police, or you will be deported, and you will lose everything. We will no longer try to help you. Danny is to be made a ward of court. This child is not to leave the hospital. You requested that your sister became a secondary carer for Joseph, and she has said you need to grow up and take responsibility for yourself. Joseph will remain with foster parents. You are free to visit anytime, but if you attempt to remove Joseph from this hospital again, you will be arrested. If you attempt to remove Danny from this hospital, you will be arrested. You will appear in court in a month's time to discuss foster care and visiting rights. You must attend this hearing, or you will jeopardise your chances of ever getting Joseph back, do you understand?'

'Yes.'

'Do you agree to the terms and agreement?'

'Yes.'

Danny said goodbye to Magda and left. He was knackered himself; his mind was all over the place. He spent another half an hour trying to find the exit. Walking around in circles. Someone told him to follow the red line until it turned green, then go left, but he wound up in the geriatric ward. Then he had to take the blue line, which took him to urology. Danny tried to retrace his steps but landed in orthopaedic.

Yellow lines, blue lines, green lines, and red, merging and parallel lines. Orthopaedic, geriatric, cardiology. Passing doctors, nurses, cleaners, porters, and hospital visitors. Utter confusion. Physiotherapy, outpatients, and then back to maternity. Danny finally found a sympathetic cleaner who took pity on him and helped him escape.

15

Danny opened up his second can of special brew, it was vile, but it did the trick. He heard the distant sound of singing, if you could call it that. It sounded more like a pig being fucked as someone screeched out the remnants of an unrecognisable tune. Then it came out through the mist. As it weaved itself slowly towards him, he sang along, slowly tapping out the rhythm on the steering wheel of his mobility scooter. Then, he just seemed to fall asleep at the wheel and was heading straight into the path of an oncoming vehicle.

He really wasn't a very good driver because he kept swerving on the wrong side of the road and falling asleep at the wheel. Blanking out again, swerving, and narrowly avoiding a car. He went weaving along the road due to his condition, which he seemed to have no control over. He was heading straight towards Danny, who was sat on a bench next to a bus stop on the corner of the park. Eventually he came to stop right next to him.

'I suffer from mild narcolepsy,' he slurred as he managed to compose himself, drawing long slow deep breaths.

They sat together at the edge of the park. Danny on the bench, him on his mobility scooter. His CD player still thumping out that obnoxious music to everyone. There was a group of

German students waiting at the bus stop on a study trip, with a rather harassed looking teacher in charge of them.

'Vould you please turn zis music down a little,' he asked, so Sam turned down the music on his CD player.

'Heil Hitler!' Sam shouted, and then gave them all a Nazi salute as the wind whipped up a mist of freshly blown snow from the ground.

Danny gapped opened mouthed in shock at everyone.

Everyone heard, everyone stopped talking, no one breathed. Danny half expected to see tumble weed drift past, not a person felt the urge to laugh or snigger. Everyone was dumbstruck. Danny felt embarrassed by Sam's actions and just wanted to fly away like a bird. Fortunately, seconds later, the school minibus turned up and they all piled in the back and drove away.

Sam opened up his third can of special brew and raised it to his mouth, 'oh I love you, yes I do, and I know that you love me to. I'm your special brew,' he sang.

Danny was attempting to read a newspaper, there was an article about a police raid on a cannabis farm.

'What's in the paper, anyone been murdered?' Sam asked.

'No, just the usual rubbish. Muggings, immigration, Brexit, Cannabis farms.'

'Brexit, what's all this Brexit shit I keep hearing about all the time, Brexit, Brexit, Brexit, what the fucks that all about?'

Danny looked at him, kind of astonished, but Sam kept gawping at him with snot hanging from his nose.

'Where have you been, Mars? It's a new breakfast cereal, it's like a mix between Ready Brek and Weetabix, it's very popular.'

'Yeah well I've never seen it in the shops,' replied Sam.

There were more people gathering at the bus stop now.

'What was that you said about cannabis farms. They gonna start growing it on farms?'

'No, they shut down one, the police executed a warrant.'

'What? Why did they execute warren not for shop lifting?'

'No, a warrant.'

'What?'

'Never mind,' Danny sighed.

Danny's phone went off. One text message, just a name, an address, and the price and the quantity required.

'I'm sorry, I have to go,' said Danny. And with that, Sam drove off. Danny watched him weave drunkard down the street.

Danny reached the top of the street and looked out at the view of the notorious condemned tower block. Not many people lived here anymore, except the junkies, and a few squatters. But Danny remembered when he was a child it was a nice place. He remembered a time when wild ponies would have stood grazing on the grass verges.

Back in the day, you could pick up a pony for the price of a round of drinks, or cheaper. People would take advantage, only to realise later to their cost that they couldn't afford to look after them properly. The poor wretches. So, there was a lot of neglect and you would find a lot of poor, skeletal, half-starved horses with deformed hooves staggering in front of cars. All over the city they used to roam. Danny remembered how the kids used to race them across the parks, down the back streets and back alleys. It was a veritable wild west in the nicest sense of the word. Now, the only horses you find in the streets are the names of pubs.

Pulling away a piece of torn wire fencing, Danny squeezed through a gap in the fence and on to the old estate. The roads were filthy and there were burnt out cars on the grass verges which had been set alight by joy riders, just beyond the wasteland where the horses used to graze.

The whole site was condemned, and it was earmarked for demolition so they could build yet more unaffordable housing. The walls were sprayed with graffiti, most of the windows or doors ever smashed or boarded up. But there were no rats, simply because rats demanded a higher standard of living.

Danny went around the back of the building and saw a mountain of old mattress. Fridges, washing machines, and all manner of broken household furniture. It seemed to be alive as pigeons were nesting within the nooks and crannies of electric heaters and old ovens. Danny could hear them cooing and see them perched in groups on top of the wreckage, strutting around, and beating their wings. Most of the debris was covered in a thick crust of blackish grey bird droppings, dried hard by the sun. They watched Danny with their piercing green eyes, their necks bobbing up and down, and some with their heads tucked right inside their bodies. Baby chicks were nesting inside an old microwave, as others hoped around aimlessly, some missing a wing, some with one foot or one eye, and some with just patches of scraggy feathers and strands of white hair sticking out, perched precariously on the rock fall of junk. Danny could see a low loader backing up to the edge of the pile lifting its tail gate and watched a waterfall of whitegoods cascade into a stream of waste. Further down a narrow alley, past some crumbling storage sheds, Danny saw a red light in one of the ground floors windows.

Danny froze as he heard voices and the sound of some smashing glass, then jumped as he saw two women emerge from an open door. He didn't know which one to focus on. He knew they weren't twins; he was just seeing double. He went inside.

Wind chimes chattered as the early morning breeze wandered through the open door. Inside the hallway, one of the adjoining doors was left wide and he could see people lying on the thread bare carpet, and old soiled mattresses surrounded by dirt. Someone lying in a foetal position, groaning loudly, one had a needle sticking out of his arm, another had a tourniquet wrapped around his thigh and was slapping his groin red raw looking for a vein.

Danny didn't feel safe. He had heard all the terrible rumours about this place, about sex crazed whores and their twisted appetites. About people asphyxiating to death during saddo masochistic sex games. But he needed to be here.

Finally, he had arrived at the address.

After Danny rung the bell, he had to wait five minutes before it was answered. Danny could hear him sliding bolts and clicking locks and chains. It took two minutes for him to undo all the locks on the door. He looked like your typical hippy and stared at Danny with his spaced-out eyes.

'Julian?' Danny asked.

'Who wants to know?' He replied.

Danny looked around and behind him, but he couldn't see anybody else standing on the doorstep and then he looked back at him scratching his balls. 'I have your order, your package?' The lights were on, but nobody was home. 'Your weed, stupid?'

'Oh, tis I pray entre,' he ushered Danny in, dramatically.

Danny followed him inside and he showed him into his flat. He offered Danny a seat and some herbal tea which he accepted, strangely enough. While he was crashing about in the kitchen, Danny waited.

His living room was quite small, but tidy, and he had a lot of nice pictures on the walls. It looked as if he had painted or at least tried to paint some of them himself. He had a lot of strange ornaments and bronze figurines of animals, like frogs, and toads. He also had a goldfish bowl on a table in the corner of the room.

'Sorry I didn't answer the door straight away, I was meditating,' he shouted.

'In bed, you sure you were meditating?' Danny said, more out of nervousness, really trying to relax.

'Best place for it, more comfortable.'

'How long do you meditate?'

'Every day, eight hours.'

'Sleeping?'

'No, meditating. Transcendental. Do you realise how hard it is to meditate properly? It takes so much concentration and it can be painful and exhausting, that's why I do it in bed.'

'Masturbating, not meditating.'

He came back into the room with two cups of herbal tea. Then got two small stones out of his shirt pocket put one in each of his hands sat down opposite Danny, shut his eyes, placed his palms in an upturned position, and hummed and hummed for about two minutes.

'Ummm, ummm,' he murmured.

Danny sat down and drunk his tea, giving him sneaky looks every so often and then continued.

'You got the money?' Danny snaped.

'Relax, I am creating a calm atmosphere with my boogie stones. Now, what can I do for you?'

'Fifty.'

'Aha, oh yes, I can feel it. I am taking on your pain.'

'What?'

'You are transferring your pain to me. I am taking on the pain.'

'You will be.'

'One moment, could you stand up?'

Danny stood up and Julian pushed his chair against the wall, then moved the television set across to the other wall and literally began re arranging all his furniture.

'What are you doing that for?'

'I've been having problems with my water heater.'

'So, why don't you call a plumber?'

'Don't be silly, it's because my bathroom is on the wrong side of the flat and it effects the cosmic energy fields. It's all about creating the right energy balance. If I put my bed on the left, it is directly underneath the upstairs bathroom which effects my digestion and I get the farts, so I leave it on the right. And my toilet is in the wrong place which is why I have to keep moving the furniture around to counterbalance the negative effects.'

'Money now,' Danny said, looking at the poster of a girl from the little house on the prairie running down a flowery meadow. 'Nice picture.'

'That's my security, she protects me from burglars. I was getting bored of the three horsemen of the apocalypse.'

Danny thought this guy was stoned. Then Julian reached out behind his seat at last. Danny thought, he can pay for the gear and I can leave this clown. Julian bought out a shiny bowl and a small stick, and then looked at him googly eyed, as he wound the stick around the rim of the bowl and created a long chiming sound.

'Chinese chime bowls and now I must check you out,' he said. Next, he picked up from behind his seat a long shiny metal object like a wand and waved it in front of him like Paul Daniels. 'This is a psychic instrument which measures things, you have to ask it a question and if it swings to the right it means yes and if it swings to the left it means no, and if it swings from left to right it means don't know. Go on, ask it a question.'

Danny tried to speak but he was clutching his stomach so hard from laughing, he couldn't get the words out.

'Look, you're not taking this seriously at all, are you?' Now Julian was getting a bit stroppy.

Slowly, the metal rod started to sway from left to right, then back and forth, and all over the place. 'The psychic energy fields are flowing.'

Just then, they were interrupted by the post coming through the door, so he went to get it came back and began to open them.

'Final demand, final demand, final demand. Oh shit, they're going to cut me off. Can you lend me two hundred? Fucking useless psychic frog,' he cursed, as he picked up a silver figurine of a frog and chucked it furiously across the room. 'Bloody stupid thing cost me one hundred sobs out of psychic weekly, it was supposed to bring me financial security. If they cut me off, how can I watch Porn Hub?'

He told Danny he was in debt up to his eyeballs and was afraid all his furniture would be repossessed. He stupidly thought Kermit the frog there would sort it all out. Danny felt sorry for him, along with all the poor spirits he said he shared his flat with. Trapped inside this lunatic's home, coughing and wheezing above the smoke of his marijuana. Danny had to leave. He said goodbye and never gave him the weed.

Sargent Tony Collins had been treading the beat around this town for twenty years. He had seen everything. Nothing surprised him. Unfortunately, they looked at things from the opposite side of the spectrum. Tony had been conditioned into believing that nobody could change. Once bad, always bad. It wasn't his fault. He came from a world where people only got worse, whereas Danny was more opened minded. They started talking about this and that whenever their paths crossed, and they had a few minutes to spare. They had many mutual interests. They became friends and sometimes he would let him sleep around his place. The art of talking wasn't dead with them, neither was the art of debate. They would sit in his apartment and expand on the possibilities of the universe, fill the room with discussion and observation.

Sitting in the darkness in front of the television set, magnetic forces interrupting and merging news and the views of the news with lights from cars outside ruining the picture.

When he arrived earlier that evening, Tony was watching the television. Danny didn't say anything much, neither did Tony. After a considerable amount of time had passed, they told each other more day to day events, like a careful diary that the room recorded catalogues of things. Danny talked, then Tony talked about what they thought on all subjects. Then Danny spoke about what was happening.

Tony said that he had warned Danny time and time again not to get too involved. He said Danny was putting his life in danger and he didn't know what he was getting himself involved with yet. He told Danny he should slow down.

'But why can't the police just arrest all the criminals and drug dealers and sex traffickers, they know who they are?'

'I wish it was that simple.'

'Why not?'

'It's not an episode of The Bill, you can't wrap up an investigation in half an hour and bang up the baddies. It takes time and money; you have to carry out proper investigations.'

'You need money?'

'Resources, manpower.'

'I don't understand?'

'We are watching Dimitri and his gang. We need all the evidence we can get. Cast iron guarantees that they won't get off on a technicality. We need proof, witness statements, lots of them. It's hard, do you really think any of his girls are going to testify in court? A girl tried once, we had to fish her out the river. I want to put them all away for a long time and throw away the key. They will get raided, they will go to prison, I promise. Eventually.'

'Can't you just run in there and get them to turn out their pockets?'

'You haven't been listening have you. I told you, for a start you need powers of search and arrest a warrant that can only be issued by senior officials. And only if they think we have a one hundred percent chance of conviction, otherwise it would get seriously messy. Sad thing is, even if we did send them all down, they would only set up someplace else. It's like fighting a losing battle.'

Light flashed occasionally from car head lamps as they passed outside, the beam would sweep past the window and fall across them like a pale flicker. Sometimes it would bleach the room like a negative in bright whites, all pattern and colouration would disappear and the people in the car would be complete the oblivious to the one chance of seeing them sat at the window on their dreadfully boring and meaningless journey.

Danny watched the weather girl on her satellite image of the British Isles, only he wasn't really concentrating because he felt so tired.

Danny cast his mind back to the night when they met at the hospital, him and Tony. He was concerned for Danny's safety. He believed that Danny was getting involved with some dangerous people. Tony stated his claim with assurance and laid the evidence before him. He told Danny how his birth mother had been involved with Albanian criminals and had been particularly close to Dimitri. These people are manipulative and cunning; they never recognise the rights of others. They appear to be charming and friendly, but they are covertly hostile and domineering, seeing other people merely as an instrument to be used and abused, and disposed of like a piece of rubbish.

Grandiose and pathological liars. They don't see others around them as human beings but as targets and opportunities. They are callous and lacking in any kind of empathy for their fellow man, feeling only contempt for other people's feelings of distress and are always ready to take advantage. Oblivious and indifferent to the devastation they cause and the lives they destroy.

'You've helped a lot, you helped made my life a lot simpler. You did well, but you should back away now. Forget about Dimitri, Bobby, Aaron, and the rest of the scum. Move on, get on with your life. You can't do anything more about it.'

Danny explained the position he was in and Tony agreed to help. Danny knew the risks involved but he was fully prepared to face them. They would meet at secret rendezvous in the grounds of hotels on the outskirts of the city and share information. During those meetings sometimes Tony would talk about his mother his real mother. He explained how he knew her. He explained that she wasn't an inherently bad person, just a very sick person. He described her life and the events leading up to his birth and told Danny that he would try and help track her down if he wanted him to. Danny wanted him to. He had a name. Katarina Sharapova. No relation.

'Danny, I've done some digging like I promised, pulled in a few favours and I've managed to find out somethings. It's not much, but it's something,' he pulled out a piece of paper from his pocket and handed it to Danny. 'Fancy a trip to the seaside? Your mothers in Sussex.'

Headlight flicked into the room and made their short journey from one side of the room to the other all distinguishable pattern and colouration obliterated.

'Tony.'

'Yep.'

'Why did you join the police force?'

'Well, to start with, I suppose I wanted to stop all the robbing, mugging, raping, and mindless violence.'

'And have you managed to give it all up yet?'

It was ten o'clock by the time Danny went.

16

The following morning, Danny was in the high street, chatting to the regulars, to the broken-hearted men and women who were living by night and hiding from the day. They all had a story to tell. How they once had a lover who left them for another so now, they wander alone in hell. Men haunted by their pasts living in doorways trying to remember better days, a long time ago when people stopped to pass the time of day. Some had been shat on and spat on. Some raped and abused. Many knew they were dying but they needed to beg for the money to escape from living inside their heads. A vicious circle.

Sweeping around the corner, he saw Phillip licking the inside of a cake bar he had just fished out the bin. Phillip had been on the streets twenty years. Nobody knew much about him, he kept himself to himself. He didn't go up the centre. He just spent all day lying on the bench or being sick. It was a miracle he wasn't dead. It was a miracle half of the street people weren't dead.

Four people slept outside Mc Donald's. Next door neighbour, Stellica, sat drinking a cup of tea in the doorway of Marks and Spencer's. He always kept his doorway nice and clean, which was more than could be said for the others, who always left their cardboard cups of urine and empty food wrappers and the occasional syringe which Danny had to deal with very carefully and dispose of in a yellow sharps box.

'Sorry, Stell, I've got to take your cardboard. New rules. Everyone's got to get out of the doorways with their belongings before eight otherwise they all get chucked.'

'OK, easy come, easy go. I get new cardboard anyway, everything wet. It not so bad, I am used to this hassle.'

'How can you be used to this?'

'I was in military, I used to sleeping outside, peoples very generous giving me money. I don't ask. Not so bad, I don't have to pay monies for board and lodgings.'

'Why don't you get a tent and go up the camp?'

'Peoples steal my stuff. You can't trust any of those peoples on the camp.'

'You need anything?'

'No, I don't need your money. I have enough, no pay bills or rent, I am free.'

'Free?'

'I had flat, didn't like. Felt like animal in cage. This is simples. I go soon London, start job construction. I know London, they have room for me.'

'Great,' He looked down at his hat which had a few donations thrown in. It didn't amount to more than a few pounds. 'How much money do you make?'

'Not as much as, Magda. She makes more money than anybody else, she makes good money.'

'How come?'

'She wakes up in morning, starts at station. By the time she gets here she has fifty pounds in her pocket, but she spends it all on shit.'

'Fifty?'

'Maybe more. Why should she work, she gets people's money? Woman pregnant live on street, peoples feel sorry.'

'She's going to work at the packhouse.'

'No way.'

'Yes way.'

'I see her yesterday in park with man smoking joint, she lies to you my friend.'

'What man?'

'I don't know, maybe her boyfriend, Yury.'

Danny picked up his cardboard, folded it under his arm, and walked back through the arcade towards the cardboard crusher. Then he saw him standing next to a bin unzip his flies and he started to urinate up the wall. He wasn't shy about it, he pulled out his plonker and shook it about oblivious. A young woman on her way to work had a look of abject horror on her face. Danny was going to have to get a scrubbing brush and disinfectant.

'Hi, baby,' said Magda.

Danny put down the cardboard against the wall. She stood arm in arm with some man Danny had never seen before who was beaming from ear to ear.

'Cold last night, where did you sleep?' Danny asked.

'With jack,' she replied. Jack grinned.

'Thank god,' Danny said and breathed a sigh of relief. He didn't care who she was staying with, as long as she wasn't in the tent. Then she gave him a long massive bear hug, squeezing his whole body in a vice like grip. She was pressing so hard against him it activated the transmission on his radio, so wherever everyone happened to be on site, every guard and every cleaner heard.

'Oh, I love you so much, baby, thank you for everything.'

'I love you.'

Then she let go. Danny heard a lot of sniggering on the radio.

'Go again, last caller,' someone said.

'Nothing, over,' Danny replied.

'Oh, I thought you said you loved me?'

'No.'

'Why don't you love me?'

'Hey!' There was laughter from the control room.

Suddenly, Magda shoved some apples and oranges into Danny's pockets. 'This man doesn't eat enough fruit,' she told jack, who had stopped smiling.

'I stay withs jack, no sex, just sleep. I get job, packhouse. I work three months, I give pay slip council, they find me home.'

'Well done, I'm very happy.' Danny wished it was that simple.

'They ask me be manager. I say no thank you, just packing, no stress. Maybe three month me manager, I get flat this is not impossible.'

'Lomax fruits?'

'Yes, sunday day off, maybe you take day off Sunday? We go carboo- OWCH!' Magda clutched her stomach, 'constant pain, this is not good.'

'You should go to the doctors.'

'No, no, no time. Just job. I strong woman! Owww.'

'Magda, the doctor said you shouldn't start work until you were fit enough.'

'One question, yes or no. I spend all my money on Joseph,

can I borrow five pounds?'

'Yes,' Danny reached in his pocket and gave her five pounds.

'Thanks, I pay you back when me pay. I pay you back everything, one year, I promise.'

They both went off passing Ella Riley, who was heading towards him from the opposite direction. She looked hot and annoyed, dressed in a Lycra vest, out for a jog. 'You dropped this!' She said and shoved a piece of paper into Danny's hand.

Danny had known the girl for a year or more, or at least he thought he had. Who can say they really *know* someone? Smiley riley, people called her. Always thinking of others before herself. That's why it was such a shock it was mild, and Danny had never seen her in a jogging vest. Her body was red and covered in goose bumps, but there was something else. Her arms and shoulders were covered in tiny razor blade scars, about an inch long. Then she put her arms behind her head and revealed even more as she stood before him and did some stretching exercises. There must have been a hundred of them, maybe more, inch-long white scars glistening in the sun. Danny couldn't see underneath the vest, thank god. There could have been even more. What happened to the girl? He fixed her stare and tried not to look. He didn't want her to see that he noticed, even though she wasn't hiding them. They were there for the whole world to see. You think you know someone. She carried on jogging. Danny looked at what she gave him. A handwritten note on a piece of lined paper, torn from a book. It read:

Keep doing the same thing and expecting different results is insanity. Don't jeopardise your recovery stick with the winners.

Danny picked up the cardboard and continued on. When he ran into Tommy, standing next to a bin, smoking a cigarette. He stood watching a group of about ten travellers shuffling about outside the sports shop, with bags full of sports clothes and other bits and pieces.

As he came around the corner, he saw three people heading towards him. It looked like Jimmy, Roman and Malik, but there was something different about them. the skin on the side of their faces was red raw and had what looked like white wavy lines in a swirly pattern imprinted on their cheeks and neck. Roman also had his hand wrapped up in plastic and they had covered themselves in some kind of face cream. It was to cover and treat their burns.

Danny read about it in the paper, they were attacked in the park. Someone had thrown acid in their faces and then bolted off on a bicycle. The police were still looking for him, the culprit, but descriptions were vague. Apparently, it had happened in the park late one evening while they sat drinking on the band stand.

Some kid had cycled up to them on his mountain bike and fired a water pistol at them containing hydrochloric acid. It was a terrible thing. Then, he just bolted off leaving them screaming in agony.

Fortunately for them, the band stand is only ten yards from a water fountain into which they jumped and submerged themselves. It looked like their past had finally caught up with them and retribution had been served from the dealer that they had stolen money from. They turned the corner before they saw him.

Danny's radio buzzed. 'Attention all calls signs; we have a lost child. Description, boy, five years old, name is Matthew Jones, brown hair, blue anorak, blue jeans, white trainers,' it bellowed.

The sun was low in the sky, casting its golden glow across the square. It hit the statue of the sheep on the plinth to commemorate where the old market used to be before they built the shopping centre and it cast its ten o'clock shadow.

Danny could hear somebody shouting, 'goth, goth, goth!' But as the sound got closer, he realised it was the bearded lady. She hadn't taken her medication and she was actually shouting 'fuck off, fuck off,' to all and sundry, just doing her usual thing, walking around and around in circles shouting at everyone.

Danny had dumped the cardboard and he was emptying the bins, pushing his blue trolly through the centre. He was outside Karen Millen when, out of the corner of his eye, he saw Bernice approach him. He got of his bike, leant it up against the wall, and walked towards him in his high heeled shoes, black fish net stockings, and tight-fitting red dress. He has immaculate hair and bright red nails. Bernice used to be Bernie. He used to be in the parachute regiment. He was big, six four and seventeen stone of muscle. He wore in a size twenty-two dress.

Bernice studied the dresses in the window display. 'Which dress do you like best?'

'Hard to say,' Danny replied.

'If you had to buy one for a fancy woman, which one would you choose?'

'Maybe the green.'

'Really, I like the blue, it's so much more stylish. You really need to learn more about women's fashion.'

'You're right, it's much better.'

'Be a darling and look after my bike for two seconds, I want to go in and ask if they have it in my size?'

'OK.'

Bernice went inside the shop and the bearded lady was heading in Danny's direction. 'Fuck off, fuck off,' she was shouting. Everyone ignored her as she walked past. Bernice came out the shop.

'Two hundred pounds, very reasonable,' said Bernice. She was loaded. She was the manager of a jewellery shop. 'I'll pick it up later,' she said. She then bid Danny farewell and peddled off.

Someone wolf whistled and shouted, 'alright darling.' It was Cat, with makeup smeared all over her face and her hair everywhere, staggering about like a drunk carthorse.

Danny radioed her in when she went into Primark. Security were already in Primark, somebody else was loading up a pram with stolen goods. Danny changed the bin outside the dress shop, gave it a spray and wipe, and went over to the next bin.

'What is this?' Danny saw Magda stomping towards him. Her hair was brunette, cut shoulder length. 'Tracy lesbian bitch, she says I take drugs, she complains to manager, I lose job. Shit situation my life.'

'Why, you don't take drugs anymore, you have to be tested every month?'

'Why she speaks this to boss, I good worker?'

'Why did she say this, she knows your homeless, you have a baby, you need a job, why? I hate Tracy, bitchy slag. How's your pain?'

'Terribow,' Magda replied.

Danny kept having to divert his gaze away from her, scanning the area for a little boy in a blue coat. 'OK, promise me you see the doctor? You will get another job. You're a good picker, but you need to rest to get better.'

'No, no time. Just another one job, very quickly, just pain, urghhh!'

Danny put his hands on her shoulders. 'Look, you've got three months, there are lots of packhouses screaming out for workers, you will easily get another job. Please promise me you will go to the doctor it might get worse?'

'OK, but not today. I see Joseph and Danny today.'

'How are they?'

'Beautiful,' she took out some Polaroids and flicked through the endless photographs of Joseph and Danny. She paused at one of the child with a nappy round its ankles. 'I change him, he cries, waaah! Five minutes then quiet, no one takes my children, no one.'

'No, no one.'

'I have to go to court Thursday, see probation confirmation. How I get to court? Nobody give me money for ticket. Court far away. Don't know train times,' she took out her letter from probation. It had a map attached with directions of how to get to court and the hearing dates and times. It was early so she would need to catch an early train, and then maybe a bus. It wasn't simple.

'Please, you give me money for ticket? You come with me to station, check train times, maybe you come with me.'

'I will have to work. Can you go with person from project?'

'No, me ban. No more help me.'

'Salvation Army?'

'No, me ban. No more help me'

'Why ban?'

'They ban me. Too much drink and fight, they find marijuana

159

in my locker. Just you help me, and Marta. Don't like project Salvation Army, kiss my arse.'

'But you were pregnant, you were living on the street, you had nothing, why they ban you just for this, they are supposed to help?'

'I know, just you and Marta. No one else. What time your lunch?'

'One to two.'

'You go visit Joseph with me?'

'OK.'

'You give me money for ticket? I spend all my money on Christmas presents for children, fucks sake.'

'OK, but I can't come with you. But I will find out the train times. Everything will be alright, I promise. Just get a job and stop smoking.'

'I stop, no smoke one week.'

'And in three months you will have a contract I will help you find a home. I will speak for you.'

'OK, see you lunch time, one o'clock,' Magda went.

Danny didn't know if he imagined it, but he thought she muttered 'stupid dickhead' under her breath. Danny continued on his route, on constant look out for the missing child.

Danny didn't like to criticise the project or Salvation Army for what they had done, but he did wish they could have shown a bit more backbone. He knew you had to have rules for a reason but banning her just seemed so harsh.

People were outside the sports shop looking suspicious, coming out with canvas bags full to the brim with t shirts sweatshirts tracksuits and trainers. As he stood outside changing the bin and wiping the stains of the sides, he saw Cam hanging around and begging for money.

'Excuse me, can you spare me some change please sir or madame?' He said. He wasn't aggressive in his manner and when they declined, he wished them a nice day.

Cam didn't steal from shops, he just hung around outside them. Cam was a tragic individual. He shifted around the town all day, being moved on from place to place. He would beg until he had enough money for his fix, then he would disappear to meet his dealer, then go to the council toilets or somewhere quiet to inject himself. Then, a few hours later, he would come back and beg some more. It was a vicious cycle. Cam just begged. He was always too stoned to steal, and he couldn't run for toffee. His body had become weak and feeble, and Danny didn't think he had long left in this world. His sadness was not planned, the road he went down was grey and empty, without end.

'Morning, Cam.'

'Morning boss,' he replied.

Danny gave him half a packet of cigarettes he found in the bin. 'Here you are.'

'Thank you,' said Cam. He was always really grateful for anything he could get.

'Don't forget to eat,' said Danny.

Cam should be suffering from every disease known to man. Piles from sitting on cold, hard pavements, rickets from a life-long diet of cola and chips. Aids from sharing needles, hepatitis A, B and C, from all the shit he has swallowed. He probably even has the bubonic plague from lying in rat-infested sewer pipes. And abscesses in the gums from never brushing his teeth, but he looked healthy just scruffy.

Danny knew his routine; wake up at 5:00am in the park, at 6:00am, beg outside the station until 11:00am, at 2:00pm meet the woman from the Women's Institute who buys him lunch. She likes to be seen with Cam. She likes to talk about Cam, it gives her a bit of a risqué reputation with her friends. Then will take ten pounds off her, go to the phone box, phone his dealer, scores round the back of one of the service yards, then goes back to his tent, injects, trips, wakes up, then repeat routine.

The travellers were back in town, just a few of them with their teardrop tattoos and swagger. They had their other halves in tow, and they were giving it large, swearing and spitting on the ground, and that was just the women. Their babies were in their huge prams like mini royal carriages, flashy and over the top, being paraded around like royalty. Aaron pulled a wad of bank notes out his pocket and gave his wife what looked like five hundred pounds. As she pushed the pram into Tesco's, Cam shuffled over to him and he took him to one side. Then he watched them disappear around the corner into one of the service yards. Danny carried on his rounds when he bumped into Gary.

'How's Magda?' Gary asked. He was straight to the point.

'OK.'

'She looked pissed off, maybe she needs her morphine injection. She looks like she wants to kill someone.'

'She doesn't take heroin, she's never taken heroin.'

'She has taken it. Yury gave it to her, mixed it up for her. Some boyfriend.'

'Yury, he's gone.'

'You sure. I thought I saw him with her yesterday? She was with some bloke in the park yesterday arguing about something, maybe it wasn't Yury. Yes, Yury gave her heroin. He got her started on it, arsehole. She used to be a nice happy go lucky girl, until he came along, the bastard. Totally controlled, her told her what to do, where to go, what to wear, who to talk to, who to take money off. All the dealers used her like a pawn. They knew she was good at it, they used her to use people for themselves, until she got too sick in the head. I know how it works, I used to live on the streets.'

'She's got a job, but she lost it again.'

'She never had a job in the first place, she's been up the park all week doing the usual, smoking, drinking, screaming at people. She won't get better. She will never change. She's an addict. She lies, the two go hand in hand, you know that. She can't help it, really. I don't think its malicious, she's just addicted to the lifestyle and she can't live without the drama. I don't know why you can't see it, you're not stupid. You know more about this than most, you can't see what's right in front of your nose. Wake up lad!'

Danny didn't know what to believe anymore. His radio clicked. '*Child has been found, reunited with family.*'

Outside Primark, a police car had pulled up, and Danny saw two policemen helping a woman into the back. She wasn't struggling, a shop guard was with her, pushing a pram once she was in the back of the panda. One of the policemen was trying to help him fold up the pram and put it in the boot, but it wouldn't fit. The security guard took it back into the shop, then a third WPC came out the store holding the baby and got in the back with the shoplifter. They drove away. Minutes later, Danny heard shouting.

'Fuck off, fuck off out of it, fuck off out the way! Get out the fucking way!' Cat Jessop was wobbling about all over the place, trying to ride a bicycle through the crowded street.

He could see Bernice twenty or so meters behind, chasing her in his high heels, stockings, and red dress, scattering the shoppers.

'Stop her! She's got my bike, she nicked my bike, stop her!' Bernice screamed and ran straight passed Danny.

Suddenly, his radio clicked. 'Security, she's just heading past the sky box, see if you can block her path,' they gasped for breath.

Danny heard Len panting on the other end, 'where is she?'

'Sky box just turned down station passage, you can cut her off if your quick!'

'I can't see her!'

'Just turned left towards the bus station!'

All you could hear on the radio was a lot of panting and her voice echoing down the passageways, 'fuck off out the way!'

You could also hear Bernice slowly gaining on her yelling, 'stop her, she's got my bike!'

'Turning back into the precinct, going down Punch Lane,' said Len, panting even more on the other end.

One security guard ran straight past Danny, running head on towards her, but she swerved past him. Now she was being chased through the crowds by Bernice and two security guards. The shoppers didn't know what to do as they all ran past Danny like a scene from the benny hill show.

'Fuck off out of it!' Cat continued to scream.

'Some one stop her!'

'She's just turned left down the bus station,' said a security guard. They were going around in circles.

Anticipating the next move, Danny swung his trolly around and ran with it towards Punch Lane. He then turned the corner and could see her peddling erratically towards him.

'Danny, block her path block her path,' the security yelled.

Danny ran into her path with his trolley, she was trying to avoid him, swinging left then right. Danny pushed his trolley in front of her wheels, she skidded, and her back wheel slid out. She tried to steady herself with her foot, but Danny grabbed the back of the bike. She tried to swipe him, he ducked, then the others caught him up and grabbed hold of her. They were all panting and wheezing.

'Come here!'

'Control. Cat Jessop, apprehended.'

Danny picked up the bicycle from the ground and gave it to Bernice.

'Do you want to press charges?' Len asked.

'No, darling, I just want my bike back.'

'Control, Bernice doesn't want to press charges.'

'OK, kindly escort miss Jessop off the premises.'

They lead her away, yelling and shouting. Bernice thanked Danny, then she peddled off.

17

Danny met Magda at lunch time. He saw her next to Clinton Cards, staring at the window display of cuddly toys.

'Beautiful, maybe I buy teddy for Joseph. I know nice shop sells beautiful furniture for home, nice not expensive. I go there when I lived with Yury, maybe I buy things for our home someday.'

They headed out towards the park in the direction of the baby unit.

The leaves were still falling from some trees onto the lawns, rust brown and yellow tones. But the trees, which lined the avenue, were evergreen, the birds flitted, and squirrels climbed them as the wind gently waved the branches. But Danny couldn't enjoy the view. He couldn't live in the moment, as Magda was permanently resident in his thoughts. As was Billy and his little gang of thugs, living rent free inside his head, scratching at the sides of his brain, when they were somewhere else enjoying themselves and didn't give a second thought to Danny's obsession.

'I bad Mother.'

'Yes. Yes, you are. But you can change. I won't lie to you, I will never lie to you. I'm your friend, and a real friend speaks the truth to you. I won't tell you what you want to hear, I tell you what you need to hear.'

As they walked through the park, they saw Bobby sitting on the park bench. They stopped.

'Magda, sit down,' he said, patting the space next to him. 'I want to talk with ye.'

'Sorry, no time,' she said.

They walked on, leaving him astounded. They walked past a few other addicts on their way to meet Bobby, she kept her head down. She didn't speak a word to any of them. She didn't even acknowledge them.

'Bad people,' she said.

'I'm glad you realise that. You need to grow up or you will lose everything.'

'I know.'

'I love you, but I hate what you have become. I hate what the drugs have done to you, but that's not the real you. The real you, the good you, she's still inside. It will be hard to get back, but you can do it. You can change if you really want to. You're a beautiful person, you are clever, very clever, but you have to stop, or you will never see Joseph again,' said Danny.

They reached the end of the park and walked through the underpass.

'No deportation, no way.'

'You're sick, you need help. I don't think you should stay here, I think it will be too difficult for you to get better. You should go somewhere else and start again. I will come with you, if you like?'

'I'm sorry, I'm sorry. I give you my problem, I not bad person, just up and down all the time,' she started crying again.

'Do you know why?'

'Broken heart. Why all people break my heart?'

'I won't.'

'No, you know I love your person too much. I don't know how I pay you back for everything, but I will someday.'

'I don't want money. I just want you to find a job and a home, and for you to stop using and be with your children. That's all you have to do for me, that's all I want.'

They walked up the road towards the special baby unit. When they got outside, they could see the foster carer taking Joseph out the back of her car. They were five minutes early, so they waited outside until they were allowed in.'

'Please, you help find place when I get contract. Not for me, for Joseph. Talk to, Amy, maybe she give me more time.'

'OK.'

'He's my son, not her son.'

'I know, nothing will change that,' said Danny, as she was crying and sobbing into him.

'They think I bad person.'

'Look, you're crying. It shows you care. You are here, some mothers wouldn't care, they would just leave him. They know you care but they don't know how hard it is. They all live in a nice home with a husband and a good job, it's much harder for you. But you will show them, you will show them all. I believe in you. You can do this. It is not impossible. Dreams can come true.'

'Maybe.'

They went inside. Danny was lying asleep in his carrier and Joseph was playing in the corner of the room with a toy car.

'Huh! What's happened to his face?' Magda cried. Tears

streamed down her face, as she gazed at Danny, who had a couple of scratches on his cheeks.

'It's alright, don't panic. He just scratched himself whilst feeding,' said Amy.

'I have milk, warm in my bag. I want give him feed,' she sobbed.

'I'm sorry, Magda, he has to be feed at specific intervals.'

'I no understand, specific interviews?'

'In-ter-vals. Special times of the day.'

'I sorry, my English not so good. I try.'

'It's alright, Magda, don't worry. He's alright, babies scratch themselves all the time,' Danny said.

'You can wake him up and change him in ten minutes, if you like?'

'I have powder cosmetic I buy. Danny, come in?'

'Sorry, no, we don't know him.'

'I know his person, he's my son, why I can't decide.'

'It's okay, I understand the rules,' Danny replied. He then said goodbye to Magda, Danny, and Joseph, and headed back to work.

As Danny walked through the subway, he spotted someone. He was sitting with his back against the underpass wall and had his knees tucked up beneath a long coat, with only his feet sticking out the bottom. It made him look like a midget. Danny sat down next to him and watched all the legs moving past them.

'Are you new, not seen you around here before?' Danny asked.

'I've been away, lived here all my life,' he replied.

'Danny?'

'Mick?' Danny shook his grubby hands.

'I saw you with Magda earlier, you a friend of hers?'

'Yes.'

'Watch yourself, she's-'

'What?'

'I dunno, tricky. I met her when I was a volunteer down the Salvation Army. We chatted, got to know each other. Then I bumped into her outside work. Everybody said I wasn't supposed to talk to the clients, that's what they called them. They gave us a big list of rules in a pamphlet called 'understanding boundaries.' They said we shouldn't get emotionally involved.'

'Right.'

'One day I saw her searching through the bins for dog ends, so I gave her a fag. She gave me a kiss on the cheek, harmless enough.'

'OK.'

'Then next day, I saw her in town, and she asked me for some money for a cup of tea. They said at the sally I shouldn't give them any money, but it was just one pound.'

'Harmless,' said Danny.

'Yeah. Then she started running into me every day, and it was money for tea, or coffee, a big mac sometimes. We enjoyed each other's company. Then one day, I didn't want to give her any money, but she got angry and started screaming at me so I gave in. Then it was every day, ten pounds for a Mc Donald's, twenty pounds for a new pair of shoes, or a cheap dress. I felt trapped. I didn't feel safe anymore. I was always looking over my shoulder, just in case she was there. I didn't like to go out anymore. She always found me. She was like that Chinese bloke

170

on the pink panther.'

'Kato?'

'She used to jump out on me, she was like a heat seeking missile. I was handing over every penny I had. Soon I was handing it over before she even asked, hundreds of pounds a month.'

'Did you tell anyone?'

'No, I felt ashamed. I felt stupid, because I couldn't deal with the situation, because I couldn't say no. She got pregnant, but she wanted an abortion, so I paid for her to go private. I thought she loved me, but she was just conning me. I know I can see it clearly now; it was all about the money. I couldn't think straight, I couldn't cope anymore. Everywhere I went, she was there. She used to spend it all on weed and legal highs. I would meet her in the park, give her money, and then she would leave me sitting on the bench. She said she would only be five minutes, she wanted to talk to someone. But I would still be there sitting on the bench an hour later. Then I would find her sitting with a bunch of dope heads, laughing at me. I told her all my secrets, I trusted her not to tell but she told everyone. One day I was in the park with her and some thug came up to me and started pushing me around and humiliating me in front of people, and she thought it was hilarious'

'Right.'

'One second, she was all sweetness, hugging, and kissing, and then all of a sudden she would turn on me and start screaming her head of calling me a wanker. I let her stay over my place for a week, but she invited all her druggie friends over and took over the place, practically. Then she kicked me out of my own home. I had to call the police when some Albanians wanted to set up shop. I upped and left town in the end, she forced me out. I gave her everything. She didn't care I lost my job with stress. We weren't even sleeping together. She said she wanted to marry me, promised she would change.'

'I'm sorry.'

'But you know what, in spite of all of that, I still love her. Despite all the drinking, drug taking, and chasing me around town all day, I was a jabbering wreck in the end. I started smoking weed and drinking myself,' he went on.

The subway was a good begging spot, there was a different person there every day. In fact, they worked it in shifts. It was a bit like pass the parcel, and the public had dropped enough parcels. It was starting to look like a bric-a-brac shop, with cardboard neatly stacked up against the wall and bags of hats, gloves, scarfs, and coats all over the place. There was another sad message written to Todd, high up on the side of the wall. It read:

Come home, Todd, we miss you. Your presents under the tree.

Back to work. There's a spike in the rubbish, gobby school kids spitting, swearing, pushing, and shoving one another. Scuffles breaking out from rival packs and rival schools. Mobile phones glued to the sides of their faces. Dropping drink cans, fag butts, crisp packets, sweet wrappers, and farts.

More school kids converging on each other, college kids, university students, all piling in, 'you're a slag!'

'Yeah you want some!'

The disabled, the disfigured, the mentally unstable drunks on mobility scooters. A dozen foreign languages, 'bonjour, guten tag, adios.' Day trippers piling of the coaches as Danny turned the corner into the bus station. A welcome ambassador in her bowler hat and umbrella being hassled by a group of Chinese tourists talking to her in Cantonese. She doesn't understand Cantonese, so they shout, still in Cantonese. Do they not understand it's like being under attack from machine gun fire? The poor girl. Along the bays, more fag butts, coke cans, plastic cups, napkins, receipts, and chewing gum. A few pennies, but he's always on the lookout for that elusive fiver, or rare ten.

Dogs are barking, kids are screaming, parents yelling, stress levels rising, dog piss running down the cracks in the pavement. But all she heard were the voices of angels in her head, above the ensuing chaos. As she stood at her alter, a rusty green metal BT electrical box, over which she had draped a blue velvet blanket, adorned with a jam jar of flowers and a photograph of the messiah, a bible in one hand, and a wooden staff in the other, dressed in a purple cloak, she quoted from the gospels. 'The lord says these are the last days, prepare yourself for the reckoning yet to come.' She scored dope on a Saturday and she saved souls on a Sunday. No one was listening. Save yourself.

Suddenly, it came speeding out of nowhere, scattering the crowd, startled by the screech of breaks, Danny froze in the path of the speeding mobility scooter. He was tensing every muscle in his body, waiting for the final impact. The driver slammed on his brakes hard and stopped two inches in front of him.

'Oh, I've got some terrible news about our Alfie. He's dead, fell through a trap door and broke his neck.'

'Oh god, that's terrible, was he doing renovation work?'

'No, they were hanging him, hah!' said Tommy. He was a proper comedian. His real name was Ian, but everyone called him Tommy on account of the fact that he reminded everyone of Tommy Steele. He was a dead ringer. 'Just seen that girl of yours, pissed out her head, yelling and screaming at someone. You've got big problems mate, wouldn't want to be in your shoes.'

'She's not really my girl.'

'I know. She must have had the baby, what colour was it, green?'

'No.'

'I know that, I mean what colour, black or white?'

'White.'

'Ginger hair?'

'Can't really tell.'

'Could be Prince Harry then.'

'Might be.'

'Where is it?'

'They're gonna put him in to foster care, she's allowed to visit, but they've got her jumping through hopes. She's got to sort herself out. They're gonna drug test her regular so she's got to stay clean, get a job, find accommodation. If she gets into trouble with the law again, she will lose everything. Get deported.'

'I admire you, for what you did for her. You tried to help, but I'll think you're an idiot if you let her move in with you. You'll have hell to pay. I won't judge you, do whatever you like, but she will put you through hell. I know what I'm talking about. My wife, she was a whore and a drunk. Stuck with her twenty years. Gotta go,' Tommy swiftly moved off, sounding his hooter.

The clothes shops, shoe shops, bookshops, and food stores are beginning to shut. The cleaners, the managers, shop floor workers, bank clerks, and kitchen porters are going home or having a fag break.

'Turned out nice again.'

'Weathers cheered up.'

Friendly people, miserable people, condescending and stuck up people who sneer at you like you can't count to ten.

When Danny came around the corner, he could see her high up on the city wall, on top of the roof of the mobility shop screaming, shouting and yelling down to people in the street below. She was listening to her headphones, dancing and waving her arms about wildly. She was with Bobby and Aaron. She'd been smoking something. Danny didn't know what. Then she spotted him.

'Hey! Sexy arse! I love you!' She pointed at Danny with both arms, swaying her hips in time to the music. 'I love you baby waah!'

Bobby and Aaron were both laughing their heads off. It was the end of a long day, nearly time to go home, when Danny got a call on his radio.

'Danny, can you go into the West Yard and sweep up some rubbish. The wind has knocked a bin over, and it's gone everywhere.'

'Received.'

The wind had started to gust, and the litter was flying all over the place. There was no point in chasing it around. Danny went into the West Yard and could see that one of the large wheelie bins had fallen over. Paper bags were flying all around him.

Clutching a large bin bag, he started grabbing the rubbish out the air, and plucking it up off the ground, cramming it into a sack. Large plastic bags were flying through the air and whizzing around like mini tornados, flying over parked cars, landing on the windscreens, and getting lodged under the tyres. The yard backed onto some shops and each unit had its individual bin. The hairdresser's bin had blown over, as had the clothes shop. The bags were not tied up, so all the hair had split, and strands were blowing all over the yard. It was impossible. Most of the rubbish was blowing towards the metal gate which lead to a secluded bin yard. Danny went over to the gate, opened up a bin, and started shovelling the paper inside. That's when he saw it.

Why do people always scream in films when they see a dead body? It wasn't Danny's natural reaction. His whole body stiffened, and he didn't have the breath in him to even speak as the full impact of the shock took hold of him and put a tight grip around his throat.

Danny just sat down back against the bin. Paper blowing around Cam's head and piling up over his body. Danny didn't know what to do. He saw the needle in his arm. His lips, tongue, and fingers had turned blue. His head had swollen up like a balloon, foam was coming out of his mouth, and his eyes were clouded over.

Danny was numb with shock. He pressed the transmission switch on his radio. But he didn't speak. He couldn't speak. His voice had been taken from his body. He pressed again. 'kccch kccch,' it was a bit like sending Morse code. He heard someone speak.

'Go again, last caller, you're all broken up, can't hear a word.'

'kccch kccch,' still no words.

'That you, Gerry?'

'No.'

'Danny?'

'Con-control.'

'Yes, go ahead.'

'Con- urgh!' Danny let go of the radio and threw up all over himself. He could still hear them trying to contact him.

'Danny, are you OK down there?'

But he was still spilling his guts over his lap. Danny grabbed the radio. 'Control!'

'Yes, go ahead.'

'Can you come down to the West Yard, there's a problem.'

'Can you elaborate?'

'OK. I've found a body. Looks like Cameron McDonald.'

'OK. Don't move.'

As they walked into the bin yard, they saw his lifeless body. His limbs were a geography of black and blue marks, dirty brown yellow bruising, a broken jaw, eyes wide open, hair flapping in the draft. Ted knelt down to touch the side of his neck. He was cold and clammy to the touch. He put his ear to his chest to see if he could hear his heart beating. Nothing. He was gone. Ceased to exist. He had left this mortal coil.

They couldn't disguise the shock they felt on their faces.

'OK, we called the police. I don't know, but they might want to talk with you. But it doesn't look suspicious,' said Ted.

'You don't need to be a detective to work out what killed him,' said Len.

'I only spoke with him a few hours ago, he was fine. I think he got some gear of a traveller.'

'Which one?'

'Can't be certain.'

'We can get it on camera if we run the tapes, what time?'

'About one o'clock.'

There wasn't much anybody could say, they just waited for the police to arrive. An hour later, the small courtyard had been taped off. Cam was zipped up in a black body bag and taken away in the back of a van.

18

They walked through the park, past the castle, over the road, and then under the subway. Then followed the stream of headlight traffic up the main road until they reached the Industrial Estate. They found a narrow alley way between Bensons for Beds and Toys "R" Us. Then they climbed through a gap in the fence, clambered over a large log, and walked down a narrow path which ran waist high through nettles and brambles, treading over plastic bags, beer cans, and bottles for about one hundred yards, twisting through the woods.

There was a beautiful golden sun on the horizon above the tree line, far away to the west. It was still winter. The rains had gone, and it was quite mild. As they walked to the campsite, they moved deeper into the woods. Danny spotted a deer. It was the most beautiful creature he had ever set eyes on.

Danny carried on under the labyrinth of black and twisted branches, deeper into the woods with Magda and Martin.

Danny tripped on a snag and he was slung forwards with some velocity. He tumbled head long down a bank, but something broke his fall because he had a soft landing.

Danny picked himself up and brushed himself down, then found himself hearing a gentle squeaking sound as he was bouncing up and down on the balls of his feet.

'Just what these woods need, an old mattress,' Danny shouted to the others, 'what should we do with it?'

'Fucking leave it!' Martin answered.

'Why would someone come all the way out here to dump a mattress?' Danny asked, bouncing up and down like Tigger.

'Maybe its Satanists, or students.'

'What?'

The other two started to walk towards him to take a closer look and began kicking it like an old tyre, pressing down on the springs.

'If they catch you, you can go to prison,' Danny said.

'This good mattress,' said Magda, as she walked around it.

'Why don't we take it to the camp?' Danny suggested, then his foot slipped, and he fell down on his backside. He just lay for a minute.

'Comfortable?' Magda asked.

'Yes, it's really comfortable. The best bed I've ever slept on!'

'Liar, we not leave here, we take back camp. I not like rubbish in my garden, maybe students use for sex. Ugh. I clean this mattress, then give people.'

Danny grabbed the corner of the mattress and turned it up on its side. It left a near perfect imprint on the grass. Nettles, a few bugs, and insects, scurried from underneath. There was a small wet patch, but apart from that, it was in good condition. No holes and no springs sticking out. It had a tiny label written on it saying 'Bensons for Beds.' They had found themselves a practically brand-new double mattress.

'I think it belongs to Bensons for Beds,' Danny said. It may have seemed like they were in the middle of Epping Forrest, but in reality, they were just in a large wooded area between the railway line and a large industrial estate. If you were quiet, you could hear the trains go past. Bensons for Beds had a large warehouse, only two hundred yards away from them.

'Not Bensons. Mine,' said Magda.

'Damaged stock.'

'Bensons don't just dump their damaged stock in the woods behind the warehouse,' said Martin. He wasn't completely stupid.

'How do you really know?'

'It's big, it won't be easy lugging it all that way.'

There were three of them, so they tried to move it. Danny stood at one end, Magda in the middle, and Martin on the end. They dragged it a few inches with effort.

'I can't get a tight grip on it. It keeps slipping.'

'I don't want to know about your sexual problems,' said Martin.

'Ugh!' They tugged and heaved trying to get a grip, but it was damp, so their hands kept slipping off.

They managed to drag it up the mound and on to the path, but before they could get it over the top, they toppled over themselves in the process and were all panting heavily.

'Leave it,' said Martin. He started to walk away.

'No,' said Magda.

'We can't carry it by ourselves,' Danny said.

'I not Wonder Woman, you man or child. You go, I never speak with you again.'

'Promise?'

'Dickhead.'

'OK,' Martin reluctantly walked back.

'If you two lift up the ends, I can crawl underneath it hold it up. Then we can try to raise it and balance it on our heads, it may be easier,' said Danny.

The others managed to lift the ends a couple of feet off the ground, Danny got on his hands and knees and crawled underneath, taking most of the weight on his back. Then he raised it up using his legs, while the others steadied it.

'Have you got it?' Danny asked.

'Yes, oh, aaah!' It slipped from their grip, Danny slipped underneath on some wet grass. He nearly did the splits, then he felt his legs click.

'Aaah!' It suddenly went very dark. He landed awkwardly underneath the mattress and was flattened at an uncomfortable angle. It was crushing him, and he could hardly breath.

'Get it off, please! Get it off!' Danny screamed. But all he could hear was laughing and giggling in that dark space.

'Should we lift it up?'

'Yes!'

'I'd rather leave him, let's go to Wetherspoons.'

'Come on, I'm trapped, I can't breathe!' Danny shouted. Suddenly, he heard screaming, then the screech of brakes, and then a ringing bell.

'Get out the road, get out the road!' Someone on a bicycle shouted, hurtling towards them.

Danny felt an almighty weight land on top of him. 'Fuck! Aaah!' Then the sound of crashing metal. 'Urgh, my fucking back!'

'Shit, my fucking bike!' said the rider.

Danny could feel someone standing up and walking all over him.

'Owww!' He screamed once more.

'What the fuck are you doing, you could have killed me?' said the rider.

'Craigie boy?'

'Martin, Mags?'

'Get me out, get me out!' Danny screamed. He was in a very uncomfortable position and his arse was getting very wet. 'Come on, guys, please! What the fucks going on, you're using me as a trampoline, get me out, it's not funny anymore!' Danny was losing air, and his back and legs were killing him.

'Who are you?' Martin asked.

'It's Craigie boy, you know, Craigie! He used to work in kitchen at centre, remember?'

'No.'

'Yes, he used to dance like chicken. Bwaah, bwaah!' Magda was clucking and crowing like a chicken, trying to prick Martins memory.

'Bwah, Bwah!' They all laughed and danced around like chickens.

'You remember, you dance like chicken and keep looking at me all the time. Why you not come back kitchen?'

'I work at the hospital. Kitchen porter.'

'Good pay?' Martin asked.

'Seven fifty, minimum. But it's enough to live on. Maybe I could get you a job?'

It went quiet for a while, then Danny heard the sound of metal banging and a bicycle being wheeled over, then someone spinning a wheel. Then he felt someone prodding the mattress.

'It's OK, mattress no damage.'

'Are you stoned?' Martin asked.

'No,' he replied.

'I remember, you proper pot head, got asked to leave for smoking weed in the toilet.'

'Bollocks, that weren't me.'

'You were weaving all over the place.'

'I didn't expect to run into idiots carrying a mattress through the woods.'

'Well, it gave you a soft landing. You like some weed?'

'I don't smoke weed. Well, sometimes. Just a little stress. Stress of work. I sometimes envy you lot. You got no responsibilities, it's free living rough under the stars with just a tent and no one telling you what to do.'

'Piss off.'

'Sorry.'

'For fucks sake! Will somebody get this fucking mattress of me, now!' Danny yelled.

'Shit, is that you, Danny?'

'Yes.'

'Get out the way you morons.' Said Craigie. Finally, they stopped jabbering and Craigie and the others lifted the mattress off Danny.

Danny saw all three of them staring down at him. He tried to pick himself up, but his back spasmed. 'Ugh! Help me up!' Danny got to his feet. His whole body felt stiff as a board.

Magda pulled an exasperated expression and raised her eyes, 'let's go,' she said.

They said goodbye to Craigie and watched him peddle off. Martin helped them reluctantly, shaking his head as they began to drag the mattress back to the camp. A full moon was trying to break through the clouds as they staggered under the canopy, trampling undergrowth, and making dead branches snap. Nits danced in the air and in their hair, making them itch. Danny saw something lurking in the misty gloom. A creature of the night. A fox or rabbit. Beside the edge of a brook they went, their legs were aching.

Forget the mattress, Danny thought.

'Bollocks,' said Martin.

'Move!' Magda shouted, as they sweated their path to the west, dragging the double mattress through the woods.

They took on a more urgent pace beside the flow of water, and now the moon had finally revealed itself and they could see far more clearly. The small brook had grown into a river. They had to stop to catch their breath.

'How much further?' Martin panted.

'Not much further, we go this way,' said Magda.

Danny wondered how she managed in her condition.

They came to a small clearing above a steep incline at the edge of a ridge and found themselves staring out across open fields. Light shifted continually beneath the clouds, casting ever changing densities of light and shade across the farmland.

Danny lent against a tree staring up into those everchanging cloud formations, stretching across the never ending grows of fruit trees, out towards the packing yards on the horizon.

They knew they were near the camp when they heard a voice calling.

'Danny!' Pavel screamed in Danny's face as he ran into them on the path, struggling with his crutches. 'I hate it here. I want to go back! I hate this country now!' Pavel took a long gulp from his bottle. He sighed, then drank some more of the lethal cocktail he had concocted and poured it into an innocent looking coke bottle, as if he could fool anybody. He looked at the ground and staggered off.

They followed him, dragging the battered old mattress behind them, down an overgrown path of tall trees and bramble until they got to a collection of tents. They were in a small enclave, set high up on a ridge above the valley floor.

Danny was surrounded by tents in a ramshackle campsite, covered with holes in the earth and soot from burnt out fires. Torn down sticks and branches and scattered across the floor with other rubbish debris. Old mugs and kettles were dumped on the earth. Then they dumped the mattress on the ground outside Magda's tent.

Some of the camp had been shopping, as they liked to call it, and were showing off their ill-gotten gains. CDS expensive jeans shirts and Vodka. Someone had even nicked some baby clothes.

The others from the camp stood in silence around a makeshift memorial that had been constructed from a couple of branches tied together with some rope in the shape of a cross. It had been made for Cam and Paulina. They mourned the passing of their friends. The anguish of Paulina's death cut deep within them. They found some flowering weeds, and they adorned the empty graveside and spread over the base of a tree. Evening was drawing in and the wind whistled around them. Some people had gathered old twigs, sticks, and bramble, and had started a fire.

Martin sat down on a log by the fire warming himself, while the others continued to drink. Magda went over, raised a bottle of vodka, and made a toast to Paulina. After about an hour's worth of singing, most of the people packed up and left or went back to their tents, until it was just Danny, Magda, a few polish people, and a young Albanian girl. She was no more than sixteen and Danny had never seen her before. One man had a mouth organ, another a tin whistle, and shortly more singing and playing began. They were warm and friendly. They weren't normal, but Danny still cherished their welcoming spirit. The wind started shaking, the branches of the trees started snapping and cracking on the fire, the laughter, the singing, the playing. Magda's eyes wild and burning bright in the flickering flames.

Danny felt far removed from all the drinking and strange behaviour, so he left them to it and helped Magda put the new mattress inside her tent.

Inside her tent, she had the old double mattress, which was stained black at the edges, a white duvet cover and some pillows. It was comfortable enough. All she had in the world was this tent and a pile of clothes and shoes. Men's clothes and women's clothes, and baby clothes. Bottles of water, packets of biscuits, and some Actimel. A photograph of Joseph was pinned to the inside of her tent. It was heart breaking.

'Welcome, Premier Inn!' She joked.

There was a strong smell of mildew. She picked up a can of air freshener and gave it a blast. Danny watched as the spray gentle settled. He then lay beside her and listened to the patter of rain on the canvas.

'Look what's happened with my life. My family give me money, come England, new life, work packhouse. I live beautiful home, my sister stole my children and peoples stole my money, give me drugs. Everything shit. Now you know why I smoke marijuana. You stay with my person, you no go home.'

'OK, what about-'

'He not come back. If come back, I kill his person.'

Magda reached under her pillow and showed him her flick knife. Danny was a bit worried, but he trusted her.

'Why don't you go back to Lithuania?'

'No go back Lithuania, too much speak, quiet.'

'Why not, please tell me, maybe I can help?'

'OK. You know I lose child, doctor take drugs?'

'Yes.'

'I come from small town. Everybody knows my person, everybody knows about my child, everybody talk about me. Lithuania is not good place for me,' Magda just stared blankly at the top of the tent. 'This bastard kill my son. Quiet. No more speak of this,' she laid back, playing with the knife, flicking the blade in and out. 'Maybe I sick, maybe I need help.'

'Maybe,' Danny replied. His heart was hammering in his chest and he was starting to sweat.

'No like Joseph, Danny stays in hospital. Dirty, maybe infection. I his mother, I look after him. Maybe I take him from hospital, no adoption no!'

Danny looked whiter than white.

'Don't look so worry, no danger. No more speak, just quiet now, sleep.'

19

The four circular objects over the optonic said it was ten o'clock. Without realising it, Danny had been rocketed four hours into the future, in what seemed like a few seconds. The glass window of this time machine had descended between him and the rest of the bustling crowd. Nothing seemed real anymore. Nothing mattered. He was in complete oblivion.

Danny slapped the odorous stranger beside him on the back. 'Can you buy me a drink?' He slurred.

He looked at Danny as if he were shit on his shoes. 'Do you know who I am? I'm the king of this town, I am. I own these streets. Nobody is allowed around here, unless I say so. I rule these streets, I do,' he stood next to Danny with his green baseball cap, turned sideways, and exposed his large beer gut hanging from underneath his torn faded t shirt. 'I own this place, I do.'

'What's your name?'

'Don't ask me my name in public, unless you wanna get shanked.'

'Who are you?' Danny asked the idiot.

'Who the fuck are you?' He replied, blasting him with his paint stripper breath.

The glass window was no barrier against his insult. His words crushed Danny, ripping his whole happy illusion to shreds. Moving through the heaving mass of bodies, Danny found himself an empty space at the bar by the door, leading on to the stairs. The noxious smell of alcohol filled the air choking him. Leaning against one of the pillars that helped hold this stinking hole together, Danny watched them. They all dressed for the racetrack in tracksuits and expensive trainers, but they never broke into a sweat. They couldn't run a hundred yards without collapsing from a heart attack. This was their mecca; the centre of their tiny universe. He sat and watched them as they pissed all their money up the wall, while the walls around him vibrated to a heavy, ethnic, thumping beat.

'They said you was in town,' Danny said, loudly, so he could hear him over the noise.

'Who said?'

'The word was out, the word on the street.'

'How's your life?'

'They owe me everything. Arseholes. They owe me their lives.'

'What's wrong, can't you find anyone to steal a drink from?' He replied. And with that, he signalled across to the barman for service.

'I don't steal their drinks; I steal their souls. I've been here for hours. I've got better things to do than bum beer money of these ingrates. A few people wanted me to buy them a drink, one of them wanted to start a fight.'

'What's the world coming to?'

'Nothing is how it seems,' Danny replied, then took a slurp from the drink Aaron had just bought him.

'I know I'm not really who you think I am, I'm really James

Bond, license to kill,' he said with a pathetic impersonation of Sean Connery. Danny boomed with laughter, took a deep breath and gulped down some more of the revolting warm Guinness and vodka mix.

'I believe you.'

'You still living in a tent?'

'It's a good one!'

'I'm sure I could fix you up with something, if you're interested?'

'I don't have to work. Everyone works for me. Pay em a fortune, you ask anyone, they will all say there working for me, even Dimitri.'

Aaron smiled; Danny was amusing him. 'Seriously, do you want a place?'

Danny nearly choked on his last dregs of black Russian; the most revolting drink ever invented, as he tried his best to focus on him. Danny drained the glass and gave out a large belch, then signalled for a refill, then felt the floor shift abruptly under his feet.

'Danny,' Aaron shouted in his ear.

'What?'

'Do you think we will make it to heaven?'

'Heaven is just a higher level of reality.'

Billy came over and put his hand on Danny's shoulder, making him cough through the mist of vapour. He saw a couple of men who seemed to be watching them. They had been listening to their conversation and laughing. Danny stared back into their wasted faces. Albanians. There was some commotion at the end of the bar.

'Get out, you're barred!' Shouted the landlord.

'Go fuck yourself!' The idiot yelled back, as his two friends held him back trying to stop a fight from breaking out.

'Get out!' Shouted the landlord.

'Go fuck yourself!' He yelled back at the landlord, even though he was only trying to save him from being splattered all over the walls. By now, everyone was aware of the situation and he was on stage.

'You want me out, you'll have to drag me out,' he casually moved his arm along the bar, deliberately knocking his glass off the edge, sending it smashing to the ground and causing a sleeping dog to yelp and run for cover.

Suddenly, the idiot shot out a left at a complete stranger sitting at the bar. The stranger ducked, then in retaliation, grabbed the idiot by the throat and pinned him up against the wall. He let him go when he started gasping for breath. The idiot grabbed the stranger's wrists, twisted him around, pulled his arm up behind his back in a lock hold, and pushed his head into a door.

Bang!

'You bastard,' said the stranger, breaking free from the arm lock.

Then the idiot started prancing around him, holding his fists up like an eighteenth-century pugilist. The idiot started jabbing lefts and rights at the stranger's head, and he slumped back against the bar. Then the idiot tried to land a heavy right to the stranger's stomach but missed and hit the bar. He grabbed his fist in agony. The stranger shot a hard-left upper cut to his chin, then a hard right, then a left. The idiot hit back, picked up a glass from the bar, then right in the smacker. The strangers nose exploded and spattered on the barman's cheek.

The stranger held his face in agony, dripping bright red blood all over the floor.

The two Albanians honoured the invitation and walked over to him. No one tried to intervene, but both men grabbed the idiot's arms and dragged him along the crowded floor whilst being stomped and spat upon by other customers. Legs were coming at him from all directions while they cheered and hollered abuse. They dragged him all the way out to the far exit, then he was hoisted up and thrown out.

His legs buckled beneath him and he fell over the steps, splashing down into a puddle of slush. He lay there while people just stepped over him on their way in and out. He asked for help, but the only help he received was a kick in the ribs, so he lay on the ground, shivering. He tried to stand, but he slipped. Then the heavens opened up a deluge upon him.

When the rain eased, Danny went outside into the beer garden. Two men and a girl were sitting on a table outside, it was quite cold, but Danny was sweating buckets.

'You alright, my friend?'

'Nice, thank you.'

'Cushty,'

He had deep set eyes, a shaven head, and his name was Dimitri.

'This is Magda, you know her?'

She looked at Danny, he didn't know what to say.

'OK.'

'OK,'

'Uh, OK.'

'Yes, you like her,' he insisted.

'I don't know her.'

'Don't worry, everything OK.'

'You want coffees? Go get us some coffees,' Dimitri asked a bar girl in a foreign language.

Magda was looking at a man sitting by himself on the other table. You could still hear the music from inside the pub, it sounded Arabic in nature and summoned up the image of a warm Morocco breeze, blowing across the desert and over Bedouin tents. But it didn't make you feel any warmer.

'You see this man, blue shirt, tattoo on neck, keeps looking at us? I remember, I remember where I see him before. He body-guard, Prince Harry,' said Magda. Dimitri didn't say anything, he just looked puzzled. She lowered her voice as she looked at Dimitri in a dazed trance. 'What if it him, what if he the man makes phone calls? No one answer mystery number.'

She showed them the phone and flicked through her list of call history. 'Here, this one number call me six times, no persons speak. I get text last week, says he has pictures me, Harry, paparazzi. Maybe he find out about me Prince Harry, maybe have pictures me and Harry hotel. London maybe sell newspapers.'

The bar girl came back with the coffees and whispered something in Dimitris ear.

'Hmm, alright my friend, you want to make some easy money?'

'why not,' said Magda.

'I need place, you need a place, make deal. Quiet, no questions, cut you in?'

'What kind of deal?'

'I find you place, police not watch. Magda speaks, me she stays with you in flat twenty-three, Dover Street. Do me a favour, I do you a favour?' He motioned to the bar girl. 'The price for her is one hundred, but you do me a little favour, I give you little present, from me to you. Maybe a little extra. I need place nobody watching, and you need a place to live.'

'Dimitri, he my friend. No troubow, he nice man. Help me, he give me job.'

'So, think about it, I have your number. I call you, don't call me. My people find you, discuss situation. I have to go now.'

Danny left too. He could feel the bile rising from the pit of his stomach. He had no time to stop into the toilets across the street. He went running, the cubicle door slamming behind him. Then he vomited, spraying watery blood everywhere as he spun around the confined space, unable to coordinate his movements. Danny fell to the floor, banging his head hard on the edge of the toilet bowl. He lay between the wall and the toilet seat for a further hour, maybe two, slurping from a bottle of vodka as if it were orange juice.

It was getting more difficult to stomach the drink now. It was like treacle; it just wouldn't go down. Danny had to take a deep breath every time before he could swallow any, it made his stomach wrench. He knew his situation was the pit. He knew he had crossed the line of no return. He had to take down Dimitri and his little gang. Tony said they needed evidence, cast iron evidence. The only way he could get it, was to join. And in order to join, he had to make sacrifices. He couldn't do this clean and sober. Danny began to feel very drowsy.

Danny left the pub. He looked up and saw dark clouds gathering in the sky and heard a distant roll of thunder, then a crack of lightning lit up the night sky. Black clouds drifted over head and the clouds burst. Rain began to hammer down.

Within a few minutes, the streets were flooded. The howling wind and thunderclaps annihilated every other sound. The rain lashed down and the lightning struck electric blue and white.

20

Danny turned right and headed up the main highway, following the stream of traffic, headlamps, fog lights, and sounding horns. The traffic was bumper to bumper, moving at a snail's pace through the driving snow and out of town. He passed a woman in the street, a child saw her raise her skirt above her knickers, revealing her goose bump legs. She communicated through a car window. Teeth chattering and cold, she got in and drove away.

'Hello, my lovely,' Danny was glad to hear a friendly voice. 'Not seen you in the rooms for a while, everything alright?'

Danny just looked at her. He didn't say a word. He didn't have to. She knew his bones and the calcium and blood that swam around him.

'We'll walk and talk,' she said. She sensed he was troubled.

They walked together in the direction of the night shelter. The street music slowly faded to nothing, only to be invaded by hydraulic fizzing, pumping engine noises, and calls from the street.

'I want my life back,' Danny told her.

'You have a choice. You always have a choice.'

'Someone's got to help her, everyone else has given up.'

'There's a reason for that.'

'She's a good person. She just goes off the rails sometimes.'

'She's sick.'

'She was well once. She can get well again.'

'You're important too.'

As they continued down the street, the wind and the snow blew harder. There was a significant police presence tonight. Many times, the traffic had to part to let them through, flashing their lights and blaring sirens.

'You can't change people. You can't make her better. You have to walk away and look after yourself. You can't fix her, no one can fix her. She has to fix herself.'

'I know.'

'You have to stop picking her up all the time. You have to let people crumble. There comes a time when you have to admit defeat. You can't save the world. She is responsible for her life and you are responsible for yours.'

'Huh?'

'I'm sorry, I know it's hard, but you're taking on hell. Walk away while you still can. It's out of your control. You can't do anything. She will destroy you. She will suck you down with her. You will both wind up dead, trust me. It's easier for her to drag you down to her level than for her to rise up to yours.'

'I won't give up.'

'I lived with a drug addict for years and I loved him more than anyone before or since. I didn't even smoke or drink when we met. Five years later, I was…Well, you remember, when I came in.'

'Yeah, I had to step over you.'

Danny remembered it well, the first time he met Ella. He Had to step over her because she was lying flat out on the

198

floor after collapsing through the doorway of her first meeting. Danny used to make the tea at that meeting and in her first few weeks, Ella used to shake so much she would slosh her tea all over the counter, and all over him. They both decided that it would be a good idea if he only filled the cup halfway up. It didn't stop her shaking, but it saved her embarrassment and the mess. They bonded with each other from the very first time she threw her tea over him.

'But I had to walk away otherwise I was going to die. And yes, I still love him, I miss him, but I love being alive more. I was lucky I got away. You're better off without her.'

'I'm not.'

'Why not, is this more about you than her?'

'Don't psychoanalyse me.'

'I'm not, I'm your friend damn it! We look after each other! Take a good look at yourself, think about it very hard and examine your motives honestly. I don't want to lose you as well.'

At the corner of the street they parted company as she stormed off.

Danny wanted a moment of clear thought, away from the constant fears playing in his head. Then he saw her slumped by the hole in the wall, invisible to the queue of people. Senseless but stunning; that was his picture of her. She was dressed in blue torn clothes with her dreamless expression and grime smudged smile, sitting on a pile of cardboard with one shoe and holding a sleeping Baby in her arms.

She looked up at Danny.

'You OK?' She slurred. Then tears welled up in her eyes. She clenched her fists and had a look of anguish on her face that broke Danny's heart.

'Is this your Baby?'

'Just my Danny, no one else. He's my Danny, no persons take my Danny,' she said, whilst stroking his tiny head.

'You took him from the hospital?' Danny said, then sat down beside her and put his arm around her, holding her hand.

'Please, you find home for us. Not for me, for little Danny. No adoption. You find home for Joseph and Danny, Please!'

'I'm calling the police.'

'No!'

Danny spoke to her gently and took both of her hands. He told her that everything would be alright. He painted a picture for her in her mind. Visualised himself, her, Joseph, and little Danny, together in a home with a garden. He told her to trust him. He wasn't sure how he would do it, but he promised her he wouldn't let her down.

'I promise you no one is going to take your children away from you.'

'No job, no home. I have nothing. Just Danny and Joseph. No one takes them,' she said, crying and shaking. 'If take them, please gun,' she mimicked shooting herself in the head with her fingers.

Danny put his hand on top of her head and gently stroked her hair then held her tight and sat back for a while.

'Go night shelter,' she said, wiping her tears.

'That's a better idea,' Danny replied.

A Few days ago, at the night shelter, Gary, the assistant manager, found a heroin wrap in the toilet. As a result, Mary, the Manager, had gathered everyone together and laid down the law. Everyone had been interrogated about it, but nobody grassed, so she decided to shut the centre down for a few days to teach everyone a lesson. She ran this place with a rod of iron. She had to.

'Thomas, I can't see your name on the list, who let you in, Gary?' Mary said, looking through the book.

'If there is a list which says we are allowed to shit on you from a great height, fuck you about for the rest of your life, and screw you left right and centre. Says you can't have a bank account, can't apply for a job, can't even have a dentist. Yes, I'm on the fucking list!' Thomas shouted back at her.

'All we have ever done is tried to get you housed and get you off drugs. You don't give a fuck about anyone except yourself. You would be dead if it wasn't for us,' Gary answered back, with his voice breaking.

Suddenly the dog Thomas was holding started to snarl, curling up the sides of its cheeks and exposing its nasty incisors. It bolted, ripping the rope from Thomas's grip, then slammed right into the Boxer and sunk its teeth into the side of its neck. The Boxer yelped as they rolled on top of each other. It wouldn't let go, sinking its jaws in further, going for the jugular and drawing blood. John still had his Boxer on the lead, and it was getting wrapped up around them both as the two dogs rolled all over the floor. John let go. Then the doorbell rang.

When Magda and Danny got outside the night shelter, it was very late. They stood shivering in the cold air waiting for the door to be answered, but nobody came to the door. Danny tried again, then Magda passed the baby to Danny and pressed the bell, keeping her finger on it.

'Tyson, Tyson!' Thomas kicked his dog hard in the backside. It still wouldn't let go. He kicked it in the side, and it let go for a second, then twisted around snarled at its owner, then the Boxer dog sunk its jaws into the striped Pitbull's rump. Soon, they were latched onto each other again, rolling around under the tables, snarling, growling and spitting blood on the floor. Both dogs were of equal size and equal measure; pound for pound all muscle and teeth. All the time the front doorbell kept ringing.

Eventually, Mary answered, looked at them both and shouted, 'Gary!' Gary came to the door, he was assistant manager, but looked more like a rough sleeper himself. 'You haven't registered Magda, you know the rules, you are supposed to register!' She continued.

'Register, what is this?'

'Your name in the book at the main centre, you know the rules.'

'Kurwa! Please let me in, I'm hungry and tired. Maybe I die. It cold, fuck sake, freezing! Please, warm inside.'

'No rules are rules,' said Mary.

'For fucks sake!' Danny shouted. He never lost his cool. 'Let her in, what you think this is a cabbage patch doll?' He said, pointing to the baby sleeping in Magda's arms.

'Maybe we could bend them just this once,' said Gary.

'No. Rules are rules.'

'Please, why you not help us,' Magda tried to push past them both, but Mary forced the door shut. Magda put her finger on the door again.

'Stand back! No one come near, get back! Get back!' Thomas hollered their leads, getting more tangled up with the dogs.

Everybody moved back. Gary was doing his best to calm the situation down. The clients had a lot of respect for Gary because he used to be like them once. Mary went into the office to call the police.

Finally, the dogs let go of each other. The owners got control of their animals and their leads. They were finally separated. After what seemed like an eternity, Gary and Mary answered the door.

Danny stood with his arm around Magda, trying to calm her down as she was crying and shaking with the cold.

'Please, I stay here tonight you know my person, I good girl, sorry I no sign book.'

'There's no room, sorry. You can't stay here, go to camp,' said Mary.

Magda grabbed Danny's arm. 'Please Danny, say something!'

Gary looked at Danny and shook his head. Magda grabbed Gary's arm.

'Please let go of my arm,' Gary said calmly, but she kept hold.

John left the building with a whimpering Boxer beside him, opening the door wide in order to get past the group huddled at the door. As the door opened, an icy blast hit them like a freight train and ruffled all the posters on the boards.

The beast from the east was blowing in and dumping its snow from Siberia on them. You could hear it hammering on the windows and whistling over the roof tiles.

'Room now, Magda stay, no go back camp, too much danger, everybody Heroin! Why you not help us?'

'I've called the police,' Mary screamed. She lost control. 'There's nothing we can do for you, now go!'

'Fuck you, fuck everybody! Magda, go in,' Magda yelled as she tried pushing past them both to get inside. In the midst of the tangle, Danny took baby Danny from her arms.

Magda swung her fist at Mary's face and hit her square in the chin. Mary staggered back, then Magda rushed her, pinning her against the side of the building, pounding her head with her fists like hammers, screaming obscenities. Mary grabbed her arms and started struggling with her, they fell to the ground. Magda and Mary were having a cat fight in the snow. Gary tried to break it up and soon it was a mass bundle. It wasn't long before sirens were wailing.

Two dark figures came running across the snow. Then a police force four by four swung past the shelter gates, snow and mud spewing from under its tyres followed by yet another panda car. The four by four braked and skidded to a halt, two policemen jumped out and pulled out tasers.

Gary got up as the panda car screeched to a halt, a policeman and woman jumped out and tried to break up the two women. In the struggle, Magda struck the policeman.

'Kurwa spierdolic!' She yelled, still kicking, screaming, and flinging her arms about.

They managed to drag her off Mary. Then they closed in on Magda, pointing the tasers, screaming at her to stay down.

The other officers managed to hoist up Magda, hold her down on the car bonnet, hand cuff her, and eventually bundle her into the back of the car, all the time screaming out her baby's name. The Panda car drove off, only then did they put their tasers back in their belts.

Danny knelt down, drained upon the snowy earth, his heart pumping in his chest, clutching hold of the baby for dear life, realising he had just escaped being tasered. He felt like he was rooted to the spot, unable to move.

Mary was blooded, but at least the baby was safe, and Magda would have somewhere warm to sleep tonight, he thought.

The officer knelt down beside him and put his hand on Danny's shoulder. Danny managed to compose himself and stand up.

'I'm worried about you,' said Tony Collins.

'Are you alright, you seem lost?' Wallis asked. 'Are you OK?' She asked again, taking hold of the baby who was still sound asleep. 'Danny?'

'Yeah, just very tired. I can't cope with much more of this.'

'Tell me about it, last time I saw you here you got thumped. She's addicted to chaos. My advice to you is keep away from her, don't get involved. You're a decent chap, not like them,' said Wallis.

'What's happened to this city?' Asked Danny.

'We do manage to lock some of them up, occasionally, but they keep coming back.'

'Do you know who the father is?' Asked Tony.

'Prince Harry.'

'Right.'

'Tony, is Magda a prostitute?'

'I know there are rumours. What do you think?'

'I really hope not.'

'If I find out anything, I'll let you know.'

'Likewise.'

'She still with this Yury?' Asked Wallis.

'Think so.'

'Match made in heaven.'

'Do you ever think she can change and get better?'

'I really hope so, but this is Magda we're talking about,' Said Tony.

'You think she might get deported?'

'That would be the best thing all round. For her, for you, and us. She can get the help she needs there. There's nothing for her here, no family, no roots, just a foreign language. She won't get any better living in the woods like a wild animal, surrounded by all those other numpties.'

'Yury might get deported.'

'Good riddance to bad rubbish,' said Wallis.

'They're as bad as each other,' said Tony.

'Got to get this baby back to Hospital. Good work, Danny. Speak to you later.'

21

Danny got to Burger King at 8:10am. There were already a few people inside. Most of the rough sleepers who had been banned from Mc Donald's across the street. Danny could already feel himself starting to defrost.

Magda was arrested the night before, taken to the police station, and charged with kidnapping a minor and wilfully endangering an infant's life. She was released on bail, pending further investigations.

John was sat in the corner with his rucksack and guitar case beside him on the floor. He was talking to Richard. Danny didn't know Richard very well; he didn't go up the centre, some people didn't like to various reasons. Too many rules. Too many undesirables or just plain old-fashioned pride. Richard was a good artist, he drew pictures and sold them to the tourists. He's got a big portfolio and he was even given a small exhibition at a local gallery after the paper did an article about him. He doesn't talk much about his former life. Not many do.

They were both drinking coffees, but they never came to Burger King normally.

'What are you two doing here, have they banned you from Café Nero or are you just slumming it?'

'Didn't you know, they found shit in the coffee?' Said John.

'What?'

'Human faeces. It was in the paper. Nero, Costa, and Starbucks. They did tests and found traces of human faeces, urine, and semen in the coffee, and the thick shakes. Staff weren't washing their hands properly.'

'Yuck! You just don't want to know that, do you? We were quite happy drinking it until they had to spoil it by telling us. Mind you, I must have swallowed a ton of shit in my time, it must be such a small amount, it can't do you any harm.'

'It can, you only need a small amount. You can catch hepatitis and if you catch that you've got an eighty percent chance of dying,' said Richard.

'It's unlikely.'

'I used to work in microbiology and I'm telling you. You only need something like five milligrams in a litre of blood before you get sick,' said Richard. Danny wasn't sure if he ever worked in microbiology, but he could have.

'Yes, and bacteria multiplies. It spreads really quickly in the human body,' said John.

'It's an aggressive agent, kills all defence systems. It's not worth the risk.'

'Thanks for the advice.'

'Paradoxically, the most expensive coffee in the world is full of shit. Made from it.'

'Made from shit?'

'Not human shit, civet shit.'

'What's a civet?'

'It's an animal, bit like a pole cat. Lives in Indonesia eats the coffee beans, and then shits them out. The farmer then makes the coffee from it, supposed to give it a beautiful taste and aroma. Costs about fifty pound a cup.'

'You ever tried it?'

'Fifty pound a cup.'

Danny left them and strolled up to the counter. 'Just a coffee please, no human faeces.'

'Pardon?'

'Just a coffee please.'

Spike was leaning against the counter, his clothes, hands, and face were filthy, covered in mud and dirt. He had a new haircut, or at least it looked like he had tried to cut it himself without the aid of a mirror. He put a cardboard crown on his head to cover the damage and stuck two straws up his nose, took a deep breath and sucked them up his nostrils then breathed out and let them drop to the floor. 'Happy Christmas,' he said. He didn't know what was going on.

He put the straws back in the straw holder. Abigail, or so it said on her name tag, came back with the coffee. Spike collected his food then walked over to the seat by the window. Danny could hear a lot of commotion coming from somewhere. There was shouting from upstairs and the voice was unmistakeable.

'Your friend is upstairs,' said Abigail. 'She stole somebody else's food and ran upstairs.'

Danny grabbed his coffee and went up. When he went up and through the door, he was met with the sight of Magda standing on the table, screaming her head off at the manager, who stood below her.

'You have to pay,' he demanded.

'No why, explain my person.'

'You have to pay for the food.'

'No, this place shit. No money, this place dirty, infections.'

They saw Danny when he came in.

'Hey, baby, no Premier Inn, no hotel no like me stay.'

'No hotel?'

'Send me back camp.'

'Have you got any money,' Danny asked. He was fully prepared to pay for the stolen items and put an end to proceedings.

'Keith stole my money.'

'Keith?'

'Yes, you deaf? Keith stole my money and my clothes.'

'Why?'

'No hotel, no money, sleep in street, this shit situation.'

The manager was looking very perturbed and hassled, he kept looking at his watch and there was nobody else upstairs.

'Look I haven't got time for this, can you please help me sort this out,' he asked Danny.

'Sleep in street,' Danny said.

'Please, cold. Please, Danny, please help me. Maybe I die. Maybe stay your home? Please help me!'

'I am very sorry, but this is not my problem. I'm sick of you people clogging up my restaurant.'

'Please, please, help me end my stay camp, you a me promise. I cold, look my face red like baboon.'

Just then Danny heard two more familiar voices behind him and saw Phil and Paul from security standing behind him, zips done right up to their chins.

'Security, surprise! Why you so fat, too much eat, go diet, more exercise.'

'We get enough exercise chasing you about all day,' said Paul.

'Huh?'

'Magda, get off the table. We haven't got time for this.'

'Dickhead.'

'Thanks,' said Phil.

'Slap me baby.'

'No, I don't want to slap you.'

'You man.'

'Real men don't hit women, Magda.'

'Bullshit!' Magda wasn't playing along. she wasn't going to pay, and she wasn't going.

'Are you going to get off the table, or are we going to have to call 126?'

Papa 126 was well known to Magda. They didn't like each other.

'126 dickhead, 456 dickheads!'

Paul spoke into his radio. 'Control, you haven't seen 126 parked up anywhere, have you seen anyone available?'

'I've already called the police and I want her arrested! I'm sick of the lot of em, she should get deported.'

'One second, Magda go toilet,' she squatted and moved her knickers to one side, revealing her vagina. They smelt a pungent odour and watched the floor beneath her flood with hot yellow steaming liquid, as she pissed all over the table. It ran of the sides, splashing onto the floor. A young worker stood gawping, holding on to a pile of trays he had just bought upstairs, with an expression on his face like somebody had just stuck a red-hot poker up his arse.

'You want locking up?' Said the manager. Just then, Tony and Wallis charged through the door, sweating profusely.

'Taxi for Magda,' Danny joked. It didn't make anyone laugh. Tony stood there with his arms folded in front of him and glared at her.

'Are we going to do this the easy way, or the hard way?'

'You arrest me?'

'Do you want me to arrest you?'

'Yes!' The manager insisted.

'Yes, just one night in cell, maybe dinner also. Me no dinner, me ban Salvation Army, me ban project.'

'Is there anywhere you're not banned?' Said Wallis.

She had to think then she replied. 'Um, Burger King.'

Tony looked around at everyone, then back to Magda, then at the puddle of urine on the floor, which was creeping ever closer towards their toes, so they shuffled back. 'I think you can add here to your list,' he replied.

'Okie dokie, baby,' Magda jumped of the table and held out her wrists. 'You cuff me?'

'No need for that if you come quietly.'

'Sorry very much, baby,' she said, then kissed Danny and gave him a very long hug. 'Don't worry, baby, you my friend forever, love you very much, you not dickhead, Magda dickhead, no more troubow, I stop everything after Easter. I promise.'

'I know,' Danny said.

'Taxi's waiting,' said Tony, and they led her away.

Danny went back downstairs and sat back down with the others. It looked like it was all over for Magda, it looked like she would lose everything. She was a hopeless case, perhaps everyone was right after all. Sitting in the corner of the restaurant, he looked around and saw Adolf come through the front door and stroll right up to him.

Not now Danny thought. 'What you want?' He asked.

Adolf put his massive hands on Danny's shoulders, his

212

psychotic glare never wavering from him. He looked even bigger close up and personal, with his shaved head full of scars. The others sitting in the group knew him only too well and they looked worried.

'Hey, Adolf, we don't want any trouble,' said Spike, calmly enough, and hiding behind big John.

Then Adolf turned his attention to the scrawny little man sitting in the corner, all by himself, who had been staring at his cup of coffee for the past thirty minutes. The man who nobody spoke to. The man with no ears.

'Oi, nonce,' Adolf growled at him, 'you're that fucking nonce from the paper.'

'Ah don't know ye,' he replied.

'You're that paedo cunt. You look like a kid fiddler,' he said and towered over him and slapped him around the face quite hard.

Stephen giggled. Danny thought that was strange.

'Right, you got two minutes to persuade me you're not a fucking nonce, or I'm gonna beat the crap out of you!'

Aaron moved away from him for a moment and glared back at Danny.

'You look like a nonce, I'll give you a slap as well!' Adolf screamed.

SLAP!

It hurt. Spike laughed nervously then moved away and over to another table. Some other people in the room gathered up their belongings and left the building.

'Get your cameras out, I'm gonna beat the crap out of this nonce!' He continued shouting.

John looked at Stephen and quietly said, 'run.'

He looked seriously worried. Stephen slowly gathered up all his wares and slowly walked away.

'Fuck off, nonce! Run away you cunt, I see you again, you're dead,' he growled like an angry Pitbull.

Adolf turned to face Danny and showed him his part open fist. Wallop! Right in the smacker. 'He's a nonce! You're a nonce, you're all fucking nonces!'

Danny should have walked, but for some reason he didn't care about anything anymore. Smack! The left hand again, cracking into Danny's jaw. It stung. The room was half full of people, but nobody intervened or tried to stop what was going on. They just ignored it and hid behind each other.

'You still here? That was the left, this is the right,' Adolf clenched his fist. 'This will kill you.'

Danny held up his hands in surrender. Maybe that was a bad idea, laying himself wide open for attack.

'OK, I don't want any trouble. I'm walking.' Danny had no choice, he had to walk. 'Cunt!' Aaron muttered under his breath, averting his gaze for a few seconds.

Danny felt enormous power rise up inside him, and in that one moment, all the anger, rage, and hurt he had ever felt in his life came to fore. In that moment he snapped. He delivered a crunching knee to Adolf's privates, and he dropped like a sack of spuds. Danny stepped over Adolf's prostrate body and left.

22

D anny's phone went. He answered. It was blunt and to the point. 'Danny, this is Lucaz, you meet me three o'clock, outside chip shop, West Gate.' The phone hung up.

It was about half past two when Danny got to the chip shop. He wasn't there. The chip shop was on the corner of the road opposite the West Park, and across the road from a prestige car showroom which had brand new top of the range Jaguar cars on display, starting at fifty thousand. Danny had half an hour, so he went over to peer through the window.

'I like the red one,' said a voice. It was Marin.

Marin was a welcome ambassador for the tourist board, there were a few of them in the city. They walked around in smart uniforms with cloaks, umbrellas, and bowler hats. They gave directions to the tourists and helped in any way they could, answering questions and googling information on their mobile devices. Marin had just come off his lunch break and was heading back into the middle of town.

Marin was from the city of Puke, no joke, Puke. It was a big city in Albania. He knew everyone.

'What are you doing out here?'

Danny couldn't explain why, but he told him. Danny told him everything the whole story about Dimitri and Lucaz. He told Danny that sometimes he was ashamed to tell people he was Albanian. Sometimes he told people he was Greek instead.

'Most people couldn't tell the difference anyway. Romanian, Bulgarian, Serbian, Albanian,' he said.

Everybody lumped them all together. He was sick to the stomach with all the bad press and negative stereotypes. He said that people think we are all bad people, all criminals. It wasn't true, Mother Theresa was Albanian.

'Stop it with this nonsense, lots of us are very hard-working people that pay taxes. Like in all countries, there are some that follow the law and some which play with it. Xenophobia is taking over this country. Its propaganda to make all us Albanians look like dirt. These people are not the real Albanians. They are crazy and fucked up soldiers from the war.'

Danny didn't know much about the war he told him, but he knew it played a major role in the rise of the mafias. Marin told Danny that heroin used to be transported to western Europe from Turkey via the Balkans, former Yugoslavia. The route was closed down as a result of the conflict, so many small Albanian gangs found themselves in an ideal position to guarantee an alternative safe route through the war zone. At first assisting the Serbian warlords, but eventually growing powerful enough to take control. Their power grew and grew. He begged him to go to the police.

Danny was getting hungry, so he decided to get some fish and chips inside him. Inside he ran into Brian. Brian was an embarrassment. The expression 'you can't take him anywhere' was made for him. He had a unique talent for putting his foot in it and saying precisely the wrong thing at precisely the wrong time.

It was a busy lunch time at the city fish bar. It was the holidays, so the small crowded hot room opposite the counter was packed tightly with mum's, dads, and children.

The smell of fish and chips frying filled the air, as Danny looked at the huge menu board trying to decide what to have. Cod, plaice, haddock, or maybe skate. He never had skate.

Brian was doing his usual thing, eyeing up any half decent looking woman under fifty. He wasn't subtle about it. They were about fourth or fifth in the queue. Danny asked Brian the question.

'Do you like skate, I've never had it, what's it like?'

It was an innocent enough question, but the answer was unexpected, even by Brian's standards.

In his loud booming voice, he blurted out. 'Did you know that the inside of a skate is exactly the same as the inside of a woman's cunt!'

Danny just wanted the ground to open beneath him and swallow him up. There was a ripple of discord and accusing looks. But it was too late, he wished he had kept his mouth shut.

'A fisherman told me that on long fishing trips, they used to wrap the skate around their cocks and masturbate!'

Danny felt rooted to the spot. He heard one snigger, but not much else. The woman behind the fish bar gave him a funny look. Danny just smiled, embarrassingly. It didn't matter what you were talking about. Brian would always find the loosest connection to some filth. He had a one-track mind. An obsession. Danny thought his mind had been rotted by his online addiction to pornography. Danny tried to change the subject.

'Did you see that series, Blue Planet, on BBC one?'

'Do you know what BBC stands for?'

'Of course, it's British broadcasting company, no, corporation.'

'No, it's big black cock!'

Eventually they got served and got out. I don't think they sold a lot of skate that lunch time.

Danny sat on the wall and ate his fish and chips. He washed it down with a can of special brew. Three o'clock came. He didn't look like he sounded on the phone. He looked friendly.

A few minutes later, Danny found himself walking through the same streets as he played as a child, where he grew up. Danny was struck by its familiarity and ordinariness but despite this, he felt haunted. Something beyond the state of play affected his state of mind and motivation which he couldn't figure out.

They walked up to an average looking house in an average looking street. Lucaz rung the bell and someone let them in. The room they entered was small. Lucaz talked to a thick set, mean looking man in a foreign language. Then they went through a side door.

Danny sat down and waited along the wall. There were two three-seater sofas and a table with a selection of adult magazines. The interior door was continually opened, then shut, and guarded by two large men who never took their eyes of you. A young man came through the door and sat down next to Danny. He was dressed all in black with bleached, white, cropped hair.

'I'm seeing Zora,' he said, 'lots of girls in there, but Zora's the best, lovely she is, who are you having?'

A young girl - *Girl* being the appropriate word - came

through the door. She was a child, really, no more than four-teen. She was made up to look older than her tender years, flanked by two bigger men and the idiot who vanished with her. Danny sat alone for five minutes, listening to the faint sounds of men groaning.

When Elena came in, Danny shuddered as they went into a room. It was small and cramped with a double bed and dressing table. On the table there was box of condoms, some Vaseline, and baby wipes. Nothing else.

'Ready,' she said.

'No.'

'No?' She moved her hand between Danny's leg's, but he edged away. 'What's wrong, don't you like me anymore?'

'You're a child.'

'I sixteen years.'

'A child.'

'Me no child,' she started to undress.

'Stop, I don't want to do this!'

'Why not? Please, I have to!'

'Do you want to?'

'Doesn't matter, you handsome man,' she kissed him, but Danny edged away. 'What is this, it's stupid, you can't put dick in woman, you man! I have to make you happy for Dimitri, otherwise he angry.'

'Don't worry about Dimitri, I will tell him you made me happy. You don't have to do this, you could run away, there are places and people that can help you.'

'Dimitri give me drugs, rape me. I good person, why he rape me. This my body, why he do this. I wish this person dead. I can't leave, they find me, bring me back prisoner. One girl leave tells the police. She dead,' she started crying. 'Sorry I cry, he speaks me, I get you nice job in hotel, he lie to me.'

'Where are your family?'

'I have no one. Please, no more speak.'

'How can I help you?'

'You can't.'

'Anything, just ask.'

'Go, don't come back.'

When Danny left, Lucaz was waiting for him. He was going to drive him to his new home and explain the details.

The traffic on the one-way system was bumper to bumper, moving in sluggish fits. They drove through slush and grit which spewed out from underneath the tyres of the cars in front and splattered thick muddy flakes of brown ice along the side of his vehicle, crawling slowly in the direction of the old cemetery. After about five minutes of uncomfortable silence, Lucaz spoke.

'Are you alright?'

'I'm OK,' Danny replied. But he had a memory inside him, one he didn't want to be reminded about.

The outside temperature was dipping as early evening approached, but it was warm and comfortable inside the luxurious leather interior of the black Mercedes. Lucaz brushed a spec of dirt off his black leather jacket and reached for a bottle of vodka which lay between his seat and the gear shift. He began swirling the dregs that were left at the bottom before quickly downing it, first checking for any unwanted observers.

'How was it for you?'

'OK.'

Lucaz started singing along to the radio, very loudly, and

very badly. 'We are the champions, we are the champions,' he shouted. 'You like Queen? I know he is not a real man, but he sings good.' Then he chuckled to himself about something. 'Ha, funny, just remembered something.'

'What's that?'

'Something about this woman, Magda, you ask.'

'I'm not really interested.'

'Three years ago, I first met her, I remember she got very carried away, pulling, biting, kicking me, trying to fight me off. I not notice smoke coming up from floor where I drop cigarette on my shirt stupid. Room caught fire, Dimitri run in put out with water, very angry with me, got out by skin on teeth.'

'Shame you didn't burn yourself down with the room.'

'I nearly did.'

'Shame you didn't succeed.'

'What a nasty thing to say.'

'You're an arsehole.'

'What you say this for?'

'You're a rapist, a child rapist.'

'Relax.'

'Paedophile, child rapist!'

'You right, I am all these things, but–'

'Keeping those poor girls locked up, getting them hooked on drugs, forcing them to sleep with men!'

He slammed on the brakes and they bolted forward. They stopped outside a deserted run-down area of the city, next to a condemned building, across the street from the cemetery.

'You act strange, are you drunk, why don't you shut up?'

'I think you should be punished, go to prison, all of you! You should all fuck off back to Albania!'

'Why don't you shut up before you say something you regret. It must be very difficult for you to understand what it's like to be a real man.'

'What happened to her and that girl that went to the police, the one they found in the river, did you kill her?'

'I don't want to say.'

'Dimitri.'

Danny was getting nowhere with him, so he pulled a knife from his coat. Lucaz let out a muffled shriek of fear as Danny grabbed him put the knife to his throat and managed to pin him up against the car door.

'Start talking.'

'W-w-wait I,' he stuttered in fear.

'You?'

'I-I-'

'You make no sense,'

'I-'

'Speak English,'

'Paulina?'

'Right,'

'I, she died.'

'Come on!'

'Let go.'

'Come on!'

'You going to kill me? You crazy!'

'Did you kill Paulina?'

'Maybe.'

'Magda.'

'What of this dumb whore?'

'What happened to her?'

'I don't know answer. She just go crazy bitch.'

'Tell me!'

'She has baby, then just disappear. Gone.'

'And the child you care, what happened to the child who was the father?'

Lucaz made a grab for the door handle. The door swung open, he fell out, pulling Danny out with him onto the pavement. Lucaz punched Danny hard in the stomach and quickly got up, as Danny lay winded on the ground.

He lit up a cigarette and leaned against the car door. All Danny could do was lay there and groan.

'Shut up, woman,' Lucaz said. Danny stopped groaning. 'You really are a crazy arsehole, you lucky man. But you need keep your big mouth shut. The only reason I don't kill you, Dimitri says nobody touch you. You his son. Your mother one of his dumb whore's long time ago. He protects you some reason, I not care, I fuck you up myself. After deal next Friday, you dead.'

'Deals off,' Danny said.

Lucaz pulled his gun in front of Danny, then he started walking towards him, shaking his weapon in front of Danny's eyes.

Danny managed to scramble to his feet.

Bang! Lucaz let one off. It may have been by accident, or maybe just as a warning. It didn't matter. The bullet bounced off the wall, and then off the deserted scrap yard. Danny hid down behind the wreckage of a burnt-out car. Then he reloaded and took another shot. The bullet whistled over Danny's head and smashed an old streetlight.

Danny didn't know where to run too. He clambered through the bushes in the direction of the cemetery.

223

Danny couldn't see anything, just endless bushes and trees all around him. It was like a maze. He was trapped. Then the awful shock of a dead end came to him. He couldn't double back, go left, or right. The only way was up, literally. So, he jumped and tried to scramble over the hedge. He made it up a couple of feet. He climbed for his life. It was a tall hedge, but it felt like it was growing against a wall. Six foot up, nearly at the top. Danny was exhausted, he hoisted himself up and over, and found himself in the cemetery.

Danny ran in the direction of the Graveyard. A plan of the graveyard hung on the gate, along with long icicles which dripped water onto the ground. Danny didn't need a map. He often came here.

Danny ran through the winter snow to plot J23, past huge Celtic crosses and weather-beaten statues of angels with blackened wings, and features worn away by generations of wind and rain. He ran past the modern gravestones which were gleaming white with bold, black lettering and older stones with words worn away, covered with green moss.

He got past the giant oak tree which stood in the centre of the graveyard, black and twisted.

Lucaz wasn't far behind. He followed the trail of deep footprints left by Danny in the snow. Most of the graves were covered with a couple of inches. The tops of vases, jam jars, small gifts, and effigies were just poking through. Flowers strewn on the grave surfaces, their bright colours striking against the winter background.

Bang!

Danny heard a terrific gun blast which echoed around the tombstones, as a million starlings took flight from the bows of the oak tree in a giant black cloud that screamed above his head. He turned to see a dark figure in the distance. He ducked down between two gravestones. Then Lucaz took another pot shot.

The bullet ricocheted off a headstone and on to another like a pin ball, then he seemed to slip over in the snow and pop up again behind a cross. He reloaded and took another shot.

The bullet whistled towards Danny and smashed the effigy of Mary on his parent's grave.

Lucaz leapt up and screamed in rage and torment with a snow bitten face, waving his gun. Then he started walking towards Danny, shaking his weapon in the air.

Had he run out of bullets. The mad man was out of ammunition. He started patting himself down, rummaging through his pockets and playing with his zips, looking for more bullets.

He was preoccupied. His attention had been diverted. Danny had no time to think, he just reacted.

Danny ran towards him, grabbed him by the collar, and shoved him backwards. He watched him plunge down a slope, arms splaying everywhere, disappearing through a mist of blown snow that whipped up across the gravestones.

Danny knelt down upon the snowy ground, his heart pumping in his chest. He realised what he had just escaped. But more importantly, the dreadful truth that he had discovered about himself.

But his heart sank at the sight of the smashed effigy on his parent's grave. The shattered glass glistened in the sunshine as he knelt still and silent for a few moments. Dimitri was nothing to him. He never will be.

The wind dropped, the air felt fresh and pure, and he felt peace of mind that he was still alive. If he were to remain alive, he needed to leave town for good. For it was clear that Lucaz was after his head.

Danny ran deep into the neighbouring woods, zig zagging under the canopy of black and twisted branches. The earth was waterlogged, so he kept losing his footing. He slipped and landed in the thick mud. He got back up and tore through the trees, splashing mud, and slipped down a ditch under the hedgerow. He backed deeper into the ditch under the brambles. He buried his head into the undergrowth. He could see Lucaz searching for him, but he was well hidden. Danny was terrified. He lifted his face from the earth, his hair spread and tangled, stuck to his face from mud. Danny heard a voice shouting foreign words through the trees. A language he didn't recognise. He could hear him closing in on him, screaming.

Lucaz reached the edge of the ditch. He stood not even five feet above him. He never heard him tremble. Danny dared not breathe. He had no doubt in his mind that he would kill him. He couldn't outrun him. He would just have to wait for the inevitable.

After Lucaz gave up his search, and Danny heard no more voices, he stayed motionless for what felt like eternity. Then he climbed through the brambles and up the ditch, hands and feet grabbing on roots and vines. With scratched hands and an entirely scratched face, he slumped his body over.

23

The unmistakeable sound of a hurricane engine could be heard. It carried in the wind and soon it burst through the hazy cloud to reveal itself. The sun gleaming of its fuselage soaring higher and higher into the deep blue yonder. Its engine whirled. Obscured by the sun, it dropped its wing and peeled off to the left, swooping low, coasting through the clouds as it plummeted to the earth.

The pilot pulled back hard on the controls and lifted it from its dive, just yards from the earth, and completed the manoeuvre. It climbed higher and higher in a giant curve, then up again with increasing speed in a mighty arc. It rose above the clouds, looping the loop. Shielding his eyes from the sun, Danny watched it tail off into the distance and over the horizon.

Looking back down again from where he stood, leaning against the wall of the Hastings Quaker House, and contemplating going inside, he saw a man approaching him from across the street.

He was suited, booted and clean shaven. He had a healthy glow and his eyes where bright.

'Hello my friend.'

'Where did you get that suit? It's nice.'

'This is my best suit. Actually, it's my only suit.'

'Danny.'

'Andreas.'

'Nice to make your acquaintance.'

'Thank you, my friend. I have a place now, and a job. Just part time, but its start. Go see my grandchildren next year, they not see grandpa three years. Come inside, have some tea, it's freezing outside. No drink, twenty-three days. But who is counting, one day at a time yes?'

'Yes,' Danny guessed.

The Quaker House was surrounded by a brick wall, with a cast iron gate which enclosed a small garden. Two benches sat under the bows of some apple trees which bore fruit in summer but were now in their spring dress of white and pink blossom. On the door hung the familiar AA logo, but the door was shut to keep the wind out.

They walked along the path of wind-blown white and pink blossom like confetti, then opened the door, and went inside. The warmth hit them in more ways than one. The room had a high ceiling with a piano in the corner and a wooden floor, nicely polished. It had arched windows and a separate kitchen with a metal shutter. There was a table with two chairs at one end, and about fifty chairs set out in front of it, arranged in a semi-circular pattern. A table at the back had an arrangement of books and pamphlets, and two large banners hanging from the walls displaying the twelve steps and the twelve traditions.

Danny went up to the counter with Andreas, but his hands were shaking.

A woman was behind the counter serving tea.

'Happy Easter Andreas,' she said.

'Happy Easter! Joan, this is Danny.'

'Hello, Danny,' she said whilst pouring Andreas a cup of tea. He quickly shovelled some biscuits into his gob and brushed the evidence off his tie. 'Tea?' She asked Danny.

His hands were shaking so much. 'I'm a bit shaky,' he admitted.

'OK, I'll just give you half a cup,' she said kindly. Joan took out the largest mug she could find and filled it halfway. 'Welcome,' she said.

There were all kinds of tea on offer; green, peppermint, rose, and camomile. They had an excellent tea department.

Andreas and Danny sat down together. They drank some tea and ate some sandwiches. Danny's hands were still shaking, so he sat on them so nobody would notice. Not that it would bother anyone.

Andreas told Danny all about his new flat. He was sixty next year, but he felt like he had been given a second chance in life. He felt like he had just stepped out of a dark cave and into the sunlight. He said that for the first time in a long time, he felt hope. Everyone looked happy and well. Everyone was a miracle of recovery. Everyone had been in the same boat and escaped disaster together. They knew each other's bones.

After the hub bub had gently died down and everybody had taken a seat, George welcomed everyone to the meeting.

'Welcome everybody to this special Easter day meeting of Alcoholics Anonymous. This is an open meeting, so anybody is allowed to attend. Andreas has agreed to kick us off with the preamble.'

'Hello everybody, my name is Andreas and I am a grateful, recovering alcoholic.'

'Hello Andreas!' Everyone replied in unison. He then read the preamble.

'Thank you, Andreas,' said everyone once he had finished.

'Joan has agreed to read a passage from the big book,' said Gary.

'Hello, happy Easter everybody! I'm Joan and I'm a recovering alcohol addict. This is from page sixty to sixty-two of the book and it means a lot to me. The first requirement is that we be convinced that any life run on self-will can hardly be a success. On that basis, we are almost always in collision with something or somebody, even though our motives are good. Most people try to live by self-propulsion. Each person is like an actor who wants to run the whole show, and is forever trying to arrange the lights, the ballet, the scenery, and the rest of the players in his own way. If his arrangements would only stay put, if only people would do as he wished, the show would be great. Everybody, including himself, would be pleased. Life would be wonderful. In trying to make these arrangements, our actor may sometimes be quite virtuous. He may be kind, considerate, patient, generous, even modest and self-sacrificing. On the other hand, he may be mean, egotistical, selfish, and dishonest. But, as with most humans, he is more likely to have varied traits.

'What usually happens. The show doesn't come off very well. He begins to think life doesn't treat him right. He decides to exert himself more. He becomes, on the next occasion, still more demanding, or gracious as the case may be. Still, the play does not suit him. Admitting he may be somewhat at fault; he is sure that other people are more to blame. He becomes angry, indignant, self-pitying. What is his basic trouble? Is he not really a self-seeker, even when trying to be kind? Is he not a victim of the delusion that he can wrest satisfaction and happiness out of this world, if only he manages well is it not evident to all of the rest of the players, that these are the things he wants and do not, his actions make each of them wish to retaliate, snatching all they can get out of the show. Is he not even in his best moments a producer off confusion rather than harmony?

'Our actor is self-centred, or ego centric, as people like to call it these days. He is like the retired businessman who lolls in the Florida sunshine in winter, complaining of the sad state of the nations. The minister who sighs over the sins of the twentieth century politicians, and reformers who are sure all the world would be utopia if the rest of the world would only behave. The outlaw safe cracker who thinks society has wronged him, and the alcoholic who has lost all and is locked up.

'Whatever our protestations are not, most of us are concerned with ourselves. Our resentment, our self-pity. So selfish and self-centred that we think is the root of our troubles. Driven by a hundred forms of fear, self-delusion, self-seeking, and self-pity. We step on the toes of our fellows and they retaliate. Sometimes they hurt us, seemingly without provocation, but we invariably find that sometime in the past we have made decisions based on self which later placed us in a position to be hurt. So, our troubles, we think, are basically of our own making. They arise out of us, and the alcoholic as an extreme example of self, will run riot. Though he usually doesn't think so. Above everything else, we alcoholics must be rid of this selfishness, we must. Or it kills us.'

'Thank you, Joan,' everyone said.

'I am delighted this afternoon to welcome, Katarina, who has agreed to share her story with us. Katarina.'

'Hi everyone, I am Katarina and I am a recovering alcoholic and drug addict.'

It was a tale of abuse, prostitution, drugs, near fatal overdoses, and everything else life could dump on you.'

In her teens she was drinking, sniffing solvents, taking amphetamines, cannabis, and ecstasy. She had trouble remembering most of it. She first tried heroin when she was in a women's prison, aged twenty. It was smuggled in easily. Two years later, hopelessly addicted to drugs, she took up with a fellow junkie and moved to Bristol, where he put her on the game. He pimped her out at fifty pounds an hour, but she had a one hundred pound a day habit.

She rolled up her sleeves to reveal her arms which were covered in track marks. she took out her false teeth. She said most of her teeth had fallen out; another effect of addiction. She also had a lot of knife scars from self-harming. She had been in and out of one co-dependant violent relationship after another. She had become estranged from her family for so long and deeply regretted the fact that she never saw her two daughters grow up, despite the fact that they are now back in her life. But her biggest regret of all. She had a son and she doesn't know where he is to this day. Taking drugs and drinking all day everyday was the only way to stop the withdrawal symptoms. It was like banging herself repeatedly over the head with a hammer in order to get rid of the ache.

'It wasn't easy when I first came through the doors, but one day at a time, I haven't had a drink or drug for ten years,' she said.

A lot of people shared back. Most people's stories were not as harrowing as Katarina Sharapova. Some people had never even been arrested for pissing in a graveyard, but it didn't matter how much or how often, it wasn't a competition. Everyone had reached their personal rock bottoms.

Then Danny spoke. 'Hello, my name is Danny. I Never knew my real mother and Father. I was born on Christmas day, 1995, at St Thomas's hospital, at four o'clock in the morning.'

THE CITY CHRONICLE
April 12ᵗʰ

Police have pledged to combat modern day slavery by cracking down on criminal gangs who traffic young women and girls for sex.

Police officers across the county took part in operation Balkan Storm. Officers raided dozens of properties in the county that they believed were being used as illegal brothels.

Yesterday, four women who are from eastern Europe believed to be sex trafficking victims were rescued from a premise in the city.

The victims include a sixteen-year-old girl from Albania. They were promised jobs in hotels, but instead, were forced into prostitution and had their passports and documents taken away.

They had all been subject to serious sexual assaults by clients and traffickers. Officers raided a further three brothels in the city and detained ten Albanian nationals as part of a major investigation into organised crime in the city.

Working on information provided by the general public and tip offs from the local community, the police worked alongside the home office and immigration enforcement officers.

Several warrants were executed, and a total fifteen people were arrested and charged with operating an illegal brothel, kidnapping, false imprisonment, suspicion of rape, grievous bodily harm, and possession of controlled substances.

Women and girls believed to be victims of sexual exploitation have been taken to a government safe house.

Chief Superintendent John Keyes, who co-ordinated the operation, said:

'Tackling organised crime is our top priority. We were able to

carry out raids because, over a period of time, we were able to build up a precise picture of what was going on, thanks to information supplied by the general public and other agencies.'

The victims of sex trafficking are controlled in such a way that it is very difficult and rare for victims to give evidence. This can happen in any neighbourhood, usually in unassuming rental properties which are leased for about six months, and then moved somewhere else. Victims don't know how to get the help they so desperately need. There are often language difficulties, and in some cases, they may not even know they are being exploited and will be living in fear.

They have been brainwashed into a distrust of police and outside authorities. Due to the arrests made in the area, we have been successful in closing down a major drug dealing operation in the city which has caused deaths and misery to a large section of the community.

24

ONE YEAR LATER

Danny stood on the beach staring out to sea. The continuous noise of the waves in his ears, lapping the shore. A loud roar as they rolled in followed by a crackle as they receded back.

Swirling ribbons of black starlings, a million or more, danced against the horizon like dark ink swirling in a jar, silhouetted against the early dawn sky above the old pier. Danny watched, transfixed, at kidney-shaped murmurations, rising and falling, tumbling and swooping, in magical synchronicity.

There was an old weather-beaten boat with blue chipped paint peeling away from it and a plastic sheet over the top to keep the rain out.

The tide was halfway out, and the seaweed was wrapped around the exposed rocks on the beach like a huge green lattice weave carpet, where seabirds flapped and squawked, pecking between the rocks for food. His eyes felt sore from the salt. Danny looked around at the cliff fall extending into the sea like a long chalky pier covered in seaweed and barnacles, as he trudged up the thick green mossy carpet of seaweed with his companions beside him. He was loaded down with fishing gear and walked to the small, decrepit-looking, but sturdy, boat on the sea edge.

They walked over to the boat and took the sheeting off. Underneath were a couple of oars and some life jackets. He rolled up the plastic sheeting on the beach.

They hauled the boat across the shingle uncomfortably and into the sea. It was very cold, so they jumped in quick. They got struck by an incoming wave. It lifted the end of the boat high up, and foam encased them as they jostled about, scrapping the seabed as they pushed out with the oars.

The little vessel buffeted about up and down over the initial waves, but soon it floated out upon calmer waters and was moving as smoothly and as rapidly as a water boatman on a duck pond.

Danny was aware of the current and the tides of the sea, so he rowed determinedly. Occasionally the boat rocked more viciously, and he tasted the salty spray, but he was in control, happy and unconcerned. Soon after, the winds dropped completely, and they bathed in glorious sunshine.

He pulled the oars in and rested. It all felt very surreal here, floating in the middle of the sea in a tiny boat, so peaceful and still. A million miles away from all the chaos of his past.

Danny never spoke about the past, only the future. He had a new name now, and a new identity.

As they had been talking, they had drifted closer to the shore. The tide was turning in more ways than one.

'Beautiful day,' said Danny.

'Hopefully the fish will bite,' said Tony.

'Hopefully,' said Katarina.

A seagull swooped overhead and soared across the horizon and underneath the arch of a dissipating rainbow out to sea.

□□□

Magda walked out of her back door and climbed through the hole in the fence, an hour before sunrise emerged on the pasture. She felt the serenity of early dawn. The sky around her was a midnight blue. She watched the sun come up over the horizon, over the Druskininkai skyline silhouetted in the distance, whilst she listened to a curlew cry.

Gradually, subtle shades of colour lifted from the darkness, and the red sun burned through the clouds that rolled over head.

Magda stepped over the barbed wire fence and on to the meadow where they had been resting all night and munching at the shoots of fresh spring grass that poked through the virgin snow. One hundred or more, quiet and still, stood grazing on the edge of the Dzukija National Park.

Holding Danny in her arms with Joseph walking beside her, they began to walk through them. Not one jerked or moved its head. They passed one beautiful dark mare and past a magnificent black stallion.

Danny turned his head sideways and saw the horses. Four huddled together for protection from the elements like silent white ghosts in a silent white world, watching the breeze bluster through their manes. For a moment, all time stood still.

Slowly, the sun climbed over the tree line and the clouds parted. Still, the horses remained. But now gleaming and glistening under the glow of a shaft of sunlight that shot from the heavens.

All eight ears pricked forwards. Their dark hypnotic eyes penetrating and acknowledging. They wined and sniffed the air, snorting plumes of frozen mist from their nostrils, and jerking their heads around. They whipped their tails, and their hove's crunched in the frost all around them.

Suddenly, one broke from the herd and the rest followed, thundering across the snow, billowing clouds of white beneath their hooves. Magda could really feel her heart thumping as they raced across the farmland with such lightning speed, the wind whipping their manes and tails as they thundered past them, racing the first light of day under the burning sun and billowing clouds. Others took flight and they surged across the fields like rolling waves on the sea. And in their running, they were free, and so was she.

God grant me the serenity to except the things I cannot change the courage to change the things I can and the wisdom to know the difference. Amen.